The Fall Guy

The Fall Guy

James Lasdun

JONATHAN CAPE
LONDON

3 5 7 9 10 8 6 4 2

Jonathan Cape, an imprint of Vintage Publishing,
20 Vauxhall Bridge Road,
London SW1V 2SA

Jonathan Cape is part of the Penguin Random House group of companies
whose addresses can be found at global.penguinrandomhouse.com

Penguin
Random House
UK

First published by Jonathan Cape in 2017

www.vintage-books.co.uk

A CIP catalogue record for this book is available from the British Library

ISBN 9781910702833

Typeset in Stempel Garamond by Thomson Digital Pvt Ltd, Noida, Delhi

Printed and bound in Great Britain by Clays Ltd, St Ives PLC

Penguin Random House is committed to a sustainable future for our business,
our readers and our planet. This book is made from Forest Stewardship
Council® certified paper.

for S., in memory

One

Summer, 2012

They'd arranged to leave late so as to avoid the traffic. Matthew, trundling his suitcase from the subway, arrived at Charlie's house in Cobble Hill at seven and helped load Charlie's bags into the back of the Lexus. It was a humid evening, and by the time they were done his shirt was soaked in sweat.

They took the tunnel out of Brooklyn and headed up the West Side Highway, Charlie slowing the heavy vehicle at every intersection to avoid the speed cameras and accelerating hard for the next stretch. All the way through Midtown the lights cooperated with his progress, spreading green welcomes as if waving some dignitary through checkpoints. Not that Charlie noticed, of course, Matthew observed to himself; Charlie would never deign to notice such a trivial piece of luck.

In Harlem they exited to stock up at Fairway, filling a cart with cheeses, olives, artichokes, caperberries. At the last minute Charlie threw in some tins of Osetra caviar.

'Best thing on earth for late-night munchies . . .'

Matthew shrugged: Charlie was paying, after all.

A few minutes later they were crossing the George Washington Bridge.

'Why don't you find some music?' Charlie said.

Matthew had thought they might talk, but did as his cousin asked, selecting Gieseking's Debussy on the iPod.

'Good choice.'

After a minute though, Charlie said:

'Actually, could you find something by Plan B?'

Matthew scrolled to Plan B. Hard beats and aggressive voices mocking the rich replaced the rippling piano.

'What do you think?' Charlie said. 'Great, aren't they?'

Matthew glanced over to see if his cousin was joking, but he didn't appear to be.

'Not bad.'

'Needs to be louder though.'

Matthew turned up the volume.

They drove down the Palisades and onto the Thruway. As they passed the Suffern exit Charlie motioned with his hand that he wanted the music turned back down.

'You know that feeling when you've forgotten something?'

'Yes . . .'

'I'm getting waves of it.'

'Uh-oh.'

'But I'm not getting a fix on what it is.'

'Someone you're supposed to've called?'

'No.'

'Something to do with work?'

'Nope.'

'Family?'

'I don't think so.'

'Maybe it's just a phantom version of the feeling.'

'Let's hope.'

Twenty minutes later, Charlie slowed down and pulled onto the shoulder.

'It's Chloe's anniversary present. I bought her a bracelet. I left the fucking thing behind.'

'Shit.'

'Shit is it.'

'Can you get it when you next go down?'

Charlie shook his head.

'No. Our anniversary's this Sunday. I can't not have a gift for her. It's our tenth.'

'Well, okay. Let's go back.'

'So much for dinner at the Millstream.'

Chloe had left that morning to drop off their daughter, Lily, at music camp in Connecticut before heading back west into New York State to meet Charlie and Matthew. The plan had been to rendezvous at the Millstream Inn in Aurelia for a late dinner before going on to the house.

'We won't get in till two or three a.m. Chloe doesn't like being there alone at night. She'll be deeply pissed and I won't be able to explain why it happened without ruining the surprise.'

'Why don't I go back?' Matthew offered. 'I can get the train from Harriman and catch the late bus up to Aurelia.'

'No, no. No. Anyway, there isn't a late bus.'

'Well, I could stay in the city. Come up tomorrow morning.'

'No, this is my screw-up. *I'll* get the train down and you can drive on up and meet Chloe. That's what we'll do.'

'That's ridiculous, Charlie. Let me go back. You need to open up the house, deal with the pool. Chloe'll be much more upset if I show up without you than if you show up without me.'

'No, that wouldn't be right. I couldn't let you do that.'

'Don't be silly. Plus this way you won't need to invent a reason for being late. You can just tell her I had some last-minute hitch and couldn't come till tomorrow.'

Charlie went on protesting, but Matthew knew he'd given his cousin what he wanted: an excuse to let Matthew fetch the bracelet without it looking too much like he, Charlie, was taking advantage. It would be a matter of purely practical necessity. In due course he agreed to the plan.

At the train station he gave Matthew his Amex card.

'Don't stint on taxis. And get a decent dinner. Rucola should still be open, or go somewhere fancier. Anywhere's fine.'

'I like Rucola.'

'Also, you can sleep at the house if you like. Lupa'll be there in the morning so you can just leave everything for her.'

'Well, I have no choice. My subletter's moved in for the summer.'

Charlie looked surprised.

'Your subletter? I didn't know you'd sublet.'

'I can't afford not to, Charlie.'

'Oh. Well, great. That's great.'

'I hope so!'

'The bracelet's in the safe, which is probably why I forgot the damn thing. I never use it.'

Charlie wrote down the burglar alarm code for the house and the combination numbers for the safe.

'I'll have to kill you, obviously, as soon as you get back tomorrow,' he said, handing Matthew the scrap of paper.

'Obviously.'

'Seriously though, tear this up when you leave the house.'

'I'll swallow it.'

'And be careful at the Port Authority tomorrow. We don't want you getting mugged with a ten-thousand-dollar bracelet.'

'Maybe I should swallow that too.'

'That's gross Matty. I'll see you tomorrow.'

There was an hour's wait for the train. Matthew had a book – his father's old copy of Pascal's *Pensées* – as well as the summer issue of *Vanity Fair*. But he was distracted. After a while he realised he was actually a little upset. Not about having to go back for the bracelet, but about Charlie's apparent surprise at the news that he'd sublet his apartment.

Hadn't Charlie meant what he said when he'd invited him to stay for the summer? He could remember

Charlie's words exactly: 'Come up to Aurelia with us. You can have the guest house. We have plenty of room for other visitors. Stay as long as you like. Stay the whole summer, bro . . .' Matthew had thanked him non-committally, not wanting to snatch too eagerly at the offer in case Charlie should have second thoughts. But a week later Charlie had repeated it, more firmly: 'Chloe and I would love to have you stay for the summer. I'm going to have to be in the city quite a bit and it'll be good for Chloe to have someone around. We thought we could appoint you official cook and grillmeister . . .' Matthew had taken him at his word, appreciating the tact of the little quid pro quo. And since he had no reason to come back down to the city for the period, he'd found a subtenant to stay in his apartment until Labor Day.

Now he had to wonder if he'd misunderstood Charlie's invitation. Had his 'Stay the whole summer, bro' not been meant to be taken literally? Was it what his father would have called just a *façon de parler*?

Well, there wasn't much he could do about it if it was. He'd advertised his apartment two months ago and the subtenant had arrived this morning; a Norwegian art historian who wanted to spend her summer exploring Brooklyn and looking at paintings in the Met. Anyway, Matthew told himself, Charlie hadn't seemed upset or put out, exactly; more just surprised.

They were first cousins, he and Charlie; their mothers sisters from Providence, Rhode Island. Charlie's mother had died when Charlie was thirteen. His father, at that time posted at the Dubai office of

6

his bank, had sent Charlie to live with Matthew's family in London. The two of them had gone to the same London private school as day boys, and for a while they'd been close: brothers in all but name. Charlie's return to the States for college five years later would have been a wrench for both of them if things had continued as expected, but that had not been the case. Instead, calamity had struck. Matthew's father, a well-to-do solicitor who'd become a member of Lloyd's, had lost almost everything when the insurance giant collapsed in the late eighties. A man of unstained character until then, he'd emptied the accounts of several of his clients and disappeared out of the country, vanishing without trace and leaving a pall of bewildered shame and grief hanging like a gaseous wake over his abandoned family. In under a year Matthew, acting out in his own singular fashion, had been expelled from school after admitting to selling drugs. As for Charlie, rather than remain in the blighted Dannecker home, he had asked his father to enrol him as a boarder for the remainder of his time at the school, and with Matthew continuing his education at a series of tutors and crammers in increasingly obscure corners of London, the boys had soon lost touch with each other. A reprisal of the friendship had never been something Matthew had considered remotely on the cards, or even especially desirable. But ten years later, circumstances had brought Matthew himself to live in the States, and after some initial reluctance he had contacted his cousin.

Charlie, at that time freshly separated from his first wife and still raw from the experience, had responded with unexpected warmth, and the two had become friends again.

Still, it wasn't the same as if they'd never had a breach. And it didn't take much for Matthew to start wondering how dependable this new-found relationship really was.

He made an effort to shrug off Charlie's surprise about the sublet, telling himself he was being oversensitive, and started reading an article in *Vanity Fair* about gourmet food trucks, a subject that happened to interest him.

The train, when it finally came, crawled morosely towards New York as if in protest at having to work at this ungodly hour. Just outside Secaucus Junction it seemed to realise it was about to relinquish any further chance of inconveniencing its passengers, and came to a complete halt for forty minutes. It was past midnight by the time Matthew arrived at Charlie's house in Cobble Hill. Rucola would be closed. He was too tired to look for somewhere still open, let alone cook for himself. He was fastidious about food, and preferred to go to bed hungry than eat poorly.

He chained the door, kicked off his shoes, and went upstairs. It felt a bit strange, climbing the three flights to the guest room with no one else there. He'd never been alone in the house before, and had only been in the upstairs quarters once, when Charlie had first bought the place and was showing it off to him. The sleek fifties furnishings that Chloe collected seemed to look at him askance from their blond frames and Naugahyde uphol-stery. A baby grand in a second-floor room stood with its double-hinged lid half open, baring its antique teeth in a cringeing grin.

Charlie had said they always kept the guest bed made up, but in fact it just had a folded comforter on a bare mattress. Matthew didn't feel like hunting up a set of sheets, and went to look for somewhere else to sleep. Lily's bed, on the floor below, was made up, but it didn't seem right to sleep in a young girl's bed, surrounded by dolls and furry toys. He went on down to Charlie and Chloe's bedroom. The king-size bed stood with its gold chenille cover and rumpled satin sheets flung back. It would do.

There was a grey marble bathroom en suite, with two sinks and a brass showerhead the size of a gong in the shower. He undressed and slid open the glass door, standing under the deluge of hot rain until he felt the grime of his journey cleansed from him.

Books on global finance, climate change, Zen and Tibetan Buddhism were stacked on one side of the bed; photography magazines and paperback novels on the other. Naked, he climbed in next to the paperbacks and magazines. As he laid his head on the pillow, he caught the smell of Chloe's perfume. He breathed it in deeply. As always, it stirred a very specific emotion inside him; unnameable, but powerfully evocative of its wearer. A short, sheer nightdress with thin shoulder straps lay crumpled on the carpet below the mattress. He picked it up and held it against the light. A strand of Chloe's dark hair glinted on the cream-coloured silk. He let the garment slide down softly against his cheek, and filled his lungs again with the delicately scented fragrance.

In the morning he woke early and went down to the kitchen to retrieve the bracelet. The safe was in the wall behind the refrigerator. Unlocking the castors as Charlie had instructed, he hauled the appliance out of its berth. The safe's dial protruded at eye level from a metal door in the wall. He turned it to the numbers on the notepaper Charlie had given him. The last four digits were 1985, and when he looked again at the other numbers he realised they formed the date Charlie's mother had died. He knew Charlie had this tender, vulnerable side, but it wasn't always visible, and his feelings towards his cousin, which could sometimes be harsh, softened whenever he was reminded of it. The steel door clicked open, spilling cold air onto his forearm. Inside, in front of some stacked blocks of cash and four bottles of Cipro, was a flat Tiffany's jewel box. He took it out and closed the safe, replacing the refrigerator and relocking the castors.

Curious to see what ten thousand dollars could buy, he opened the box. The bracelet was a thick cuff of gold, with 'Tiffany & Co' inscribed along one edge. An utterly bland piece of jewellery, in Matthew's opinion. He felt bad for Chloe, about to receive something that, with her taste, she could only find banal, but which she would obviously have to pretend to like.

He put the box in his pack, and left, resetting the burglar alarm.

It was another day of clinging heat in New York. The Port Authority smelled like a dumpster. But the bus was cool inside and not too crowded, and as it headed north, the foliage along the Thruway glittered promisingly.

He picked up the article he'd been reading the evening before, on gourmet food trucks. It was a business he'd been thinking of getting into himself, some day, if he could raise the money. In London, when he was eighteen, a friend of his mother had taken him on at the trattoria she owned in Fulham, and taught him the rudiments of the restaurant business. Later, an acquaintance of the same woman had offered him a job in New York, where he'd learned to cook professionally, and one way or another food had been his livelihood ever since. A somewhat lean one in recent years, it had to be said. A curious lassitude had taken hold of him lately; a feeling of being adrift, and of not quite having the willpower to do anything about it. He'd had a share in a farm-to-table restaurant in Greenpoint that he'd sold three years earlier for a small profit, and he'd planned to reinvest the money in another, more promising venture, but he'd hesitated at the last moment; stayed home in a state of peculiar inertia on the morning of the final round of discussions, and the opportunity had passed. Since then, as if in obedience to some mysterious but inflexible organic law, his field of operations had been steadily dwindling. He blogged about food and made a little money off ads. A friend at a TV production company sometimes called him up to consult. He was registered with an agency that sent out chefs for private dinners, and occasionally he got a gig. But it was all beginning to feel rather remote – and not just the food business but other things too. Recently, he'd come across the coinage 'meatspace', meaning the real, as opposed to the virtual, world, and had found himself adopting it as his own private expression for what he seemed to be steadily, unaccountably, withdrawing from. Or what seemed to be withdrawing from him. Meatspace of worldly accomplishment. Meatspace of relationships. Meatspace of money. At thirty-nine he was close, in fact, to living off pure fumes of just about everything. It wasn't something he experienced as a great hardship, but he was aware that the moment was approaching when even the fumes would run out.

The bus stopped by the village green in Aurelia, opposite the hardware store. The place was thronged: teens playing Hacky Sack, gardeners at work on the riotously blooming plantings, tourists milling around with cameras and ice creams. Behind the clapboard and brick buildings rose the round-topped mountains of the Catskills. They weren't majestic, exactly, but they were big enough to suggest the idea of a wilderness, and to confer a bucolic air on the bustling little town. Matthew sat on a bench with his bag, waiting for Charlie.

He'd been to Aurelia several times before; weekend visits, and once over Thanksgiving. A century ago an arts colony had been founded there, and the town had been a haven for artists and musicians ever since. In their wake, these bohemians had brought an unusual combination of ragged drifters and well-heeled New York weekenders who mingled together in a curious symbiosis of mutual flattery. The weekenders were of the type who liked to think of themselves as successful members of the counter-culture, and the drifters clearly enjoyed the boosted status they got from being the real thing. Some of the stores along Tailor Street – the main thoroughfare – were head shops selling tie-dye T-shirts and drug paraphernalia, but there were also upscale realtors' offices advertising two-million-dollar homes, as well as a couple of cafés where you could get a decent macchiato, and one good restaurant, the Millstream Inn.

After ten minutes Charlie pulled up on the road behind the green, stopping in front of the white-spired Dutch Reform church. He was driving the convertible now, a cream-coloured BMW that Chloe had driven up the day before. He was dressed in a white tennis shirt and shorts. His handsome, regular features were already a little sunburned.

'I brought you something from the juice bar,' he called out, waving a tall cup at Matthew.

Matthew took the drink and got in the car. It was a watermelon juice; cold and not too sweet.

'Thank you.'

'Thank *you*, man. You saved my ass. Everything go okay?'

'Everything was fine.' He gave Charlie the bracelet.

'Thanks, Matt. Really appreciated.'

'No problem.'

Charlie grinned at him in the mirror:

'Were you surprised to see all that moolah, in the safe?'

'I didn't really look,' Matthew said. A momentary disappointment crossed Charlie's face, and it occurred to Matthew that his cousin had wanted him to be impressed by the money.

'I mean, it looked like a good amount . . .'

'One and a half mill,' Charlie said. 'Everyone was doing it after 9/11. Then the Cipro after the anthrax scare. To be honest it seemed irresponsible not to.'

'Totally irresponsible.'

'Hey, don't mock!'

'Sorry.'

'If the big one drops, you'll know where to come, right?'

'Thanks, Charlie.'

'I mean it.'

Leaving town, they wound up into the mountains. The warm air rushing over Matthew's face smelled of summer. At Charlie's road they began climbing more steeply. The road, with its hairpin twists, had been cut into the mountain in the nineties when the town first began attracting the so-called 'little millionaires' of the Clinton era. The houses along it were sleek and modern, with irregular-angled decks jutting out to take advantage of the view, stone-bordered swimming pools flashing turquoise in their grounds.

Charlie's house, on a parcel of twenty acres near the top, was an almost invisible structure in which bluestone, cedar and glass mingled with the surrounding rocks, woods and sky in an ingenious way that made you unsure, as you approached, which part of what you were looking at was natural, which man-made.

From the front there was a tremendous view all the way to the Hudson river, across what looked like virgin forest, at least in summer when the billowing foliage swallowed everything but the odd church spire.

As Charlie opened the front door, Fu, their enormous black Chow, bounded over. Matthew found the dog's slobbering friendliness hard to take, though he did his best to conceal it, letting the creature jump up against his chest in his usual over-friendly greeting, without betraying too much distaste. Charlie tried to calm the animal but Fu ignored him, mashing his wet nose and bluish-black tongue into Matthew's chin.

'We're having some issues with Fu,' Charlie said apologetically.

Stone floors and walls kept the air cool inside. Rawhide sofas and armchairs were grouped in the sunken living room around a carved wooden coffee table laden with Chloe's photography books.

Off to the side, the open-plan dining room and kitchen looked out onto the terrace and lawn through a Japanese wall in which glass doors, paper panels and wood-framed bug-screens could be arranged in combinations to let in different amounts of light and air. On the far side of the lawn was the pool, flanked by the pool house, with the guest house perched on a rock beyond.

'I'm going to take a shower,' Charlie said. 'Go say hello to Chloe. She's by the pool. Your bag's in the guest house. Everything's ready for you.'

Two

Matthew hadn't seen Chloe for a couple of months, but even if he'd seen her just a day ago, or only an hour, it would not have been a neutral event for him to see her now. It never was.

He had been trying hard, lately, to come to an accurate understanding of his feelings for her. A year or so after his father's disappearance, his mother had sent him to a therapist: a large, sombre Australian named Dr McCubbin. The sessions at Dr McCubbin's office overlooking Hampstead Heath had done little to alleviate the effect on Matthew of his father's actions, but in their own way they had been instructive. McCubbin had taught Matthew how to analyse his emotions by instilling in him the habit of asking himself: 'What does this feel like? Where else have I experienced this particular shade of joy or sadness? What specific associations does it have for me?' He'd also taught him not to be afraid of any desire or impulse he might discover by this process. The psyche, McCubbin had shown him, was autonomous. You couldn't alter its inclinations, however much you might want to, so there was no point in trying. You could, however, avoid being tyrannised by them, and the better you understood them, the easier this would be.

In the case of Chloe, Matthew had teased out a large number of disparate components in the general feeling of enchantment he experienced in her presence. Being several years older than her, he had to acknowledge something paternal in his attitude; a kind of protective, delightedly disapproving fondness that he imagined he might feel towards a daughter if he should ever have one. At the same time, as Charlie's cousin and honorary brother, he felt related to her on a more equal, sibling- or in-law-like footing. Then, in the tacit arrangement by which it was always as the beneficiary of her and Charlie's hospitality that he saw her (there was never any question of them visiting him in his dismal little one-bedroom in Bushwick), there was also something of the dependent child in his feelings towards her; or at least a projection of something parental onto her. Then too, there was that very precisely defined and circumscribed amatory interest that the medieval poets understood so well: the attraction of the squire to his master's lady; a matter of devotion on one side, and infinite kindness on the other, with the mutual understanding that any favours granted must be of a purely symbolic nature. More prosaically, he'd always felt a simple, friendly affection for her. She'd been a food photographer before marrying Charlie, and knew some of the people Matthew had worked with in the restaurant business in New York. She liked art and literature in the same unintellectual way that Matthew did, and shared his weakness for low-end celebrity gossip. The soft peal of her laughter as the two of them worked their way through the love lives of Lindsay Lohan and the Kardashians, often to the accompaniment of Charlie's snores, was a sound Matthew had come to associate with his evenings at their home in Cobble Hill, and it formed a significant part of the picture he'd imagined as he looked forward to their summer together in Aurelia. And then finally there was that sense of almost supernatural kinship that exists often between people who seem on the surface quite unalike but whom life conspires to link by a succession of small affinities, creating a bond that exists in a world of its own, requiring neither comment nor confirmation in this world.

He'd felt this bond since first meeting her, a decade earlier. Charlie and she had just started dating and Charlie, whose disastrous first marriage had left him distrustful of his own judgement, had wanted to know what Matthew thought of her. The three of them met at Charlie's old apartment in the Village. Right away Matthew could see she was in another class from the women Charlie had introduced him to previously. Her clear, structural attractiveness, her good taste in clothing that came across as a natural elegance completely unlike the over-groomed glamour of her predecessors, her quiet curiosity and absolute lack of pretension, made him extremely happy on Charlie's behalf. Charlie, who was redecorating his apartment, had just bought some Basquiat drawings, and the three of them had started talking about art. At one point Charlie had asked Chloe what her all-time favourite painting was. She'd thought for a moment, and then, as she began to speak, Matthew had known with a strange certainty that she was going to name the one and only Old Master painting that had ever meant anything to him: Bellini's *Madonna with Saints*, which his father had taken him to see in the church of San Zaccaria when they went to Venice on a trip around Europe the year before he disappeared. 'That would have to be Bellini's *Madonna with Saints*,' she'd said, and the hairs had stood up on the back of Matthew's neck. It had seemed to bring him back through the years to the moment when he'd entered the church with his father, both of them weary and surfeited from their day of sightseeing, and stood together, bound suddenly close in their silent mutual amazement at the monumental slabs of colour arrayed across the painting in the form of the saints' robes, each figure in its dissonant brilliance engulfing the two of them like some tumultuous, intensely differentiated type of joy. 'We won't forget that in a hurry,' his father had said when they finally ran out of coins for the illumination, 'will we?'

Not wanting to upstage Charlie, who hadn't heard of the picture, Matthew had restrained his reaction, merely nodding to show that he approved of Chloe's choice. But as Charlie's friend he'd felt overjoyed that the woman who was so obviously the right woman for Charlie was also, so to speak, the right woman for himself.

So now, as he went out through the glass doors across the bluestone terrace with its glazed urns of pink geraniums, over the freshly cut lawn and through the lines of young apple trees planted to conceal the chain-link pool fence, he was in some fantastical sense approaching an idealised composite in whom daughter, sister, cousin, mother, mistress, friend and mystical other half, were all miraculously commingled.

At any rate, that was the best he could do to account for the trance-like state he seemed to enter when he was with her, in which he felt simultaneously hyper-alert – as if some benign force were commanding every resource of wit, charm, sensitivity and brilliance he possessed to stand at attention – and dazed to a point of happy unself-consciousness.

She was sunbathing on a deckchair at the far end of the pool. As Matthew opened the gate she sat up and waved to him.

'Hello, Matt.'

'Hi, Chloe.'

She stood, putting a shirt on over her swimsuit and sliding her sunglasses up over her dark hair which she had knotted on top: imperfectly, so that strands fell over her face.

It was a highly expressive face, constantly in subtle motion. Her large, very dark eyes seemed to register every passing nuance of feeling with warmly mirthful intelligence.

'I'm so sorry about last night,' she was saying as she came towards him, her white shirt catching flares of light from the pool.

'Oh, no problem – all my fault anyway,' he bluffed, realising he'd forgotten to ask Charlie what reason he'd invented for Matthew's return to New York.

They kissed on the cheek, and he caught her scent again; its bittersweet notes that seemed to him so precisely emotional he barely noticed their physical qualities at all.

'Make yourself at home,' she said, motioning to the guest house. 'Then come have a swim.'

A second gate led to a path that climbed the outcropping of rock on which the guest house stood, an octagonal wooden eyrie with towering black pines behind and the abyss of the vast valley dropping almost sheerly in front.

He'd stayed there before when they'd had other guests in the main house. He loved the place. Often, when things got too much for him in New York, he fantasised about asking Charlie to let him live there full-time as his caretaker. The wide-board floors scavenged from an old sawmill, the rustic wooden walls, the assortment of furniture Chloe had picked out – spindle-backed Shaker chair, bird's-eye maple dresser, cedar blanket chest, the modern rug of overlapping green and grey squares – all appealed to him as if they'd been chosen expressly with his own tastes in mind.

He could see the pool through the window above the dresser as he unpacked his clothes. Charlie came through the far gate in his trunks, carrying an iPad. He went over to Chloe, who tilted her lips up to receive a kiss, placing her hand on his thigh. Despite his own feelings, Matthew enjoyed witnessing the flow of affection between Chloe and Charlie. He had no actual designs on Chloe, and in fact believed in her and Charlie's marriage almost as an article of religious faith. It was something he considered absolutely right and absolutely fixed. Its very solidity was precisely the reason why he was able, as Dr McCubbin would have put it, to 'experience' his own feelings for Chloe with as much pleasure as he did, with as little guilt, and with no sense of rejection whatsoever. It was actually a very comfortable arrangement, as far as he was concerned.

Charlie sat at a table in the shade of the pool house and began working on his iPad. He'd recently been let go from a hedge fund when it was bought by a company that wasn't interested in keeping the Green Energy Equities division Charlie had been managing, and he was currently in the process of trying to reposition himself as some kind of ethical investing consultant. One of the things he'd told Matthew he was planning to do over the summer was write a document – an article or possibly even a short book – that would address contemporary culture from the point of view of the socially responsible investor. 'I'll be requiring your input, bro,' he'd said, and Matthew had felt flattered, and wanted.

At breakfast the next morning, Chloe was wearing the bracelet. She held out her wrist as Matthew joined her and Charlie under the grape arbour that shaded the stone terrace.

'Look what Charlie gave me.'

He feigned the surprise expected of him.

'Isn't it nice?' she asked.

'It's gorgeous.'

'Tiffany's. Look.' She pointed at the edge of the cuff where the name was engraved. He nodded, glancing up into her eyes and then quickly away, not wanting to be complicit in anything even gently ironic at Charlie's expense.

'What's the occasion?' he asked Charlie.

'Oh. It's our wedding anniversary,' Charlie answered, pouring himself a cup of coffee.

'You should have told me. I'd have brought you breakfast in bed.'

Charlie gave a vague smile and turned to his iPad, apparently uninterested in extending the harmless charade. It didn't surprise Matthew: playfulness had never been his cousin's strong suit.

'Well, happy anniversary,' he said, raising a cup of coffee.

Later, by the pool, it occurred to him that the two of them might want to celebrate alone.

'You two should go out tonight. I mean for a romantic dinner, by yourselves.'

'Huh . . .' Charlie said, looking over at Chloe.

'No, let's just stay here,' Chloe said, not opening her eyes. 'It's so much more relaxing. Matthew can cook us all something special for dinner. Right, Matthew? We can have some nice drinks and just . . . relax. Don't you think, Charlie?'

'Actually, I do.'

'I'll tell you what,' Matthew said. 'I'll check out the Millstream's specials and give you what you would have had if you'd gone there.'

'Great,' Chloe called out from the raft she was floating on, smiling dreamily. 'Only it'll be ten times better.'

'Nice thought, Matty,' Charlie said.

They kept a pickup truck at the house, an old Dodge, for winter storms when the steep road became too icy for even the Lexus's four-wheel drive. Charlie had offered it to Matthew for the summer when he invited him, and he gave him the keys when they went back inside for lunch. It had minimal suspension; every dent in the road jolted up through the seat like a mule-kick, but Matthew enjoyed driving around in it. It made him feel like a soldier bouncing around on some important mission in a jeep.

In this particular instance the mission, diligently transcribed from the Millstream's website, entailed hunting down guajillo chillies, fresh gulf shrimp, mesquite chunks for the grill, trevisano radicchio, baby artichokes and a butcher who knew how to cut flat-iron steaks or would let Matthew cut his own. It took all afternoon, but between a farmstand twelve miles away in Klostville, the new All Natural Meats and Smokehouse on the road to East Deerfield, the surprisingly well-run fish counter at Morelli's Market in East Deerfield itself and a bodega off the Thruway near Poughkeepsie that Matthew had discovered on a previous visit, he managed to get what he needed.

The evening was a notable success. Charlie opened a 1973 La Lagune and even though Matthew wasn't much of a wine connoisseur, he had a good enough palate to appreciate the simple grandeur of the bottle. Remembering it in later days, he made the connection he'd never made before, between the word 'claret' and the idea of clarity it had originally been adopted to express. It seemed to sum up the evening. Clear evening sky. Simple perfection of the dinner as he served the appetisers and then, after a pause to let the mesquite chunks burn down, the flat-iron steaks. These, though not actually from Wagyu beef, were as good as any he'd eaten, their seared crimson flesh branchingly marbled by the infraspinatus fascia that offset the fire-and-blood carnality of the shoulder muscle itself, sweetening it with rich oils. Clear, untainted friendship between the three of them: their easy happiness together as they sat around the stone table with the citronella candles flickering in silver buckets between the terracotta herb-pots beside them, and the stars coming out in the cloudless sky.

The conversation flowed, gaining just enough of a charge from the slight tension between Charlie's stubborn high-mindedness and the more bantering style of Matthew and Chloe, to feel both relaxed and interesting. Charlie mentioned a video clip he'd watched that afternoon, of Noam Chomsky talking about the Occupy movement. Chloe rolled her eyes, good-naturedly. Placing her hand over Charlie's she asked what Noam Chomsky had had to say about the Occupy movement, and she smiled sweetly up at him as he embarked on a long answer in which the professor's opinions became inextricably entangled with Charlie's somewhat rambling commentary.

'He used the word "dyad", I remember. I had to look that up.'

'What about it?'

'Oh, something about how from the point of view of corporate power the perfect social unit is the dyad consisting of you and your screen. Pretty accurate, wouldn't you say?'

'It certainly describes you, darling', Chloe said affectionately. She was still wearing the bracelet, swivelling it in the candlelight as if to stave off any suspicion that she might not have liked it. And maybe she really did like it after all, Matthew found himself magnanimously conceding. It was entirely possible that the aesthetic fastidiousness he attributed to her was purely a figment of his own imagination. A side effect of the unspoken sympathy between them was a frequent sense of 'knowing' things about her that he couldn't objectively vouch for, and he was quite prepared to admit that they weren't always strictly accurate, and moreover that they tended to skew in the direction of certain qualities, such as 'reserve' and 'tastefulness', that certainly oversimplified her and possibly idealised her too. The gift she'd given Charlie, for example, was neither reserved nor especially tasteful: it was a Givenchy shark T-shirt, which Charlie was wearing under one of his white linen shirts, the top three buttons open so that it looked as though a shark were breaching up out of his chest. But it was certainly more interesting than the bland gold manacle he'd given her.

Charlie went on talking about Occupy for a while. The movement, which at that time was still gaining in strength, had interested him from the start. Once, when Matthew had gone to meet him at his old office, Charlie had insisted on dragging him off to the Zuccotti Park encampment. For two hours they'd ducked in and out of the tarp shelters and nylon tents, listening to teach-ins and strategy meetings, watching the 'human microphone' in action. Charlie was taking pictures on his phone and earnestly questioning the protestors, who'd been roughing it for several weeks by then and were easily distinguishable from the tourists and visitors by their dirty clothes. The little oblong park was like a raft thrown together after some great shipwreck, Matthew had thought, with its makeshift dwellings lashed down every possible way. For him the whole phenomenon existed in a realm he had long ago placed off limits to himself, a realm of faith in human betterment that he considered himself too tainted by experience to enter. His duty, he felt in an obscure way, was to preserve that realm from his own limitless scepticism.

Charlie, however, had no such inhibitions. The visit had made a deep impression on him, and he'd brought it up many times since, often wanting to show Matthew articles or YouTube clips on his iPad, frowning into the screen as he asked Matthew what he thought, or used him as a sounding board for his attempts to articulate what *he* thought.

As a banker, it had seemed necessary to him to formulate a position in regard to this movement. He seemed

28

to want to find arguments that would place it and himself in a sympathetic relation to each other. At the same time Matthew sensed that he wanted to be able to set it in a larger context that would allow him to demonstrate its flaws and contradictions, and thereby, presumably, diminish the anxiety it seemed to arouse in him.

'I was forever trying to persuade Chloe to photograph the different encampments around the country, wasn't I?' Charlie said now. He'd been going on about the movement for quite a while by this point. Drink made him long-winded, and he'd drunk a fair amount. 'I thought it would make a great project for her. Go round the country photographing all those tent cities. Right, Chlo?'

'Right.'

'How come you weren't interested?'

Chloe shrugged. Seeing the quick shadow of impatience cross her brow, Matthew mentioned something he had noticed earlier that day. He did it purely to change the subject, not wanting the atmosphere to be even momentarily spoiled.

'Speaking of photographic projects,' he said, 'I was noticing the mailboxes up here as I drove around today. They're so full of character, the way people decorate them with all those little hand-painted stars and flowers. I was thinking they were a kind of folk art almost . . . It crossed my mind that they might actually make a worthwhile project for a photographer.'

Chloe turned to him.

'That's interesting.'

29

'What mailboxes?' Charlie asked. 'I've never seen any decorated mailboxes.'

'They seem to be all over the place. Especially down the smaller roads.'

'Yes. They're everywhere,' Chloe said.

'I hadn't noticed.' Charlie poured himself another glass of wine.

'Sometimes you see a whole cluster of them.'

Chloe nodded. 'Right. At the corner of shared driveways. The mail vans don't go down private roads.'

'I saw a row of about fifteen all tilted together. They looked like a sort of drunken chorus line.'

Chloe laughed.

'Huh?' Charlie muttered.

'You know, I think you're right, Matthew,' Chloe continued, looking thoughtful. 'That *could* make an interesting project.'

She smiled warmly at Matthew. He wiped his lips with his napkin, trying to conceal the pleasure her reaction had roused in him. Actually, he was a little surprised at her enthusiasm. Having given up commercial photography after marrying Charlie, she'd become serious about pursuing it as an art, exhibiting her work in downtown galleries, and he didn't think she'd really be tempted by that kind of purely coffee-table material. He'd only raised the subject to steer the conversation away from Zuccotti Park, which had seemed to be boring her, and he'd frankly expected the idea to be politely rejected. But she appeared to be genuinely interested.

'I'll take a drive around tomorrow,' she said. 'Thanks, Matt. That was a great suggestion.'

After they'd finished eating Chloe insisted on helping Matthew clear up. Charlie, promising he'd do it next time, sprawled into one of the Adirondack chairs with a cognac, feet up on the footstool.

'I'd like to make a toast, though,' he announced, reaching for his glass. Matthew put down the dishes he'd been about to carry in. Another effect of drink on Charlie was a tendency to make toasts and speeches that could ramble on indefinitely.

'To Chloe,' Charlie began, his voice a little slurred. 'To Chloe, whom I love more than anything under the stars, I want to say . . . I want to say *thank you*. I want to say thank you for ten years of unwavering love. I want to say thank you for your . . . for your support . . . for your *patience*.' He paused, nodding slightly as if in private satisfaction at something unexpectedly judicious in the choice of word. 'I want to say thank you for the ten happiest years of my life so far. Look, I don't . . . I've never claimed to be a saint, but I think I'm a better person than I was, and if I am, if I've made any . . . if I've grown in any way as a human being I owe it to you, Chloe. You have a way of bringing out the best in people. Maybe in my case even making them better than they . . . better than their best. So here's to you, my beloved wife . . . Here's to the next ten years, and all the . . . all the next decades ahead of us. May they all be as happy as this, and full of love, and adventure, and . . . well, you know . . .' He raised his glass and drained it, and then sank back against the slats of green-painted wood.

After a moment, Chloe stepped over and leaned down, kissing him tenderly.

'I love you too, Charlie,' she said.

A look of immense contentment spread over Charlie's sleek features. He closed his eyes. Pretty soon he started snoring. In sleep, he looked older than he did when he was awake. You noticed the thick, tawny eyebrows over the closed lids, the slight lugubrious prominence of his lower jaw, the extravagant sprawl of his limbs. You could see he was destined to become one of those kingly, leonine old men who appear in ads for golfing resorts and upscale retirement communities. Without envy, with a kind of amused inner candour, Matthew often thought of himself as a member of some troll-like, inferior species when he was in his cousin's presence.

In the kitchen, Chloe told him Charlie had complained of feeling under the weather the previous afternoon, after taking Fu for a walk in the woods.

'I hope he didn't get a Lyme tick,' she said, glancing out at the terrace.

'Probably just a touch of rabies,' Matthew answered. After a moment, Chloe gave a soft peal of laughter.

He loved making her laugh. It was the one bodily pleasure he was permitted with her; a harmless physical trespass. And since they seemed to find the same things funny, he did it fairly often.

'I'm going to have a swim,' she said when they'd finished the dishes. She didn't ask Matthew to join her.

He assumed she didn't think he needed to be asked, but even if she had, he would have declined. He wouldn't have wanted Charlie to wake from his slumber on the terrace to find him and Chloe having a midnight swim together. Not that Charlie would have thought anything of it, but he himself would have, and he was dimly conscious of a need to keep himself well back from any realm in which feelings of desire or guilt might proliferate.

He said goodnight and went on up the rocky path to the guest house, navigating the last yards by the light of the moon that had risen above the valley.

From his octagonal room he could see the still, undisturbed surface of the pool, and then the dark figure of Chloe in her white T-shirt coming to the gate. Lightning bugs flashed in the apple trees as she passed through them, making the small apples gleam. As she opened the gate he closed the curtains. He thought she might swim naked and he didn't want there to be any suggestion in her mind, ever, that he could be spying on her. Still, his guess was that even alone, at night, she probably would have worn her swimsuit. She was rather American and modest in that way.

But closing the curtain had the effect of opening his imagination to the thought of her undressing at the pool's edge with the moonlight on her supple body, and as he heard her plunge into the water he felt again, more strongly than ever, the sensation of lovely clarity that had pervaded the whole evening.

Three

The summer thickened around them. Soon it reached that point of miraculous equilibrium where it felt at once as if it had been going on for ever and as if it would never end. The heat merged with the constant sounds of insects and red-winged blackbirds, to form its own throbbing, hypnotic medium. It made you feel as if you were inside some green-lit womb, full of soft pulsations.

After breakfasting, the three of them would go their separate ways. Charlie drove off early in the convertible to play tennis. Afterwards he'd take Fu for a walk in the woods, returning as often as not looking exhausted and a bit chagrined, with some tale of the ungovernable animal thundering off after a deer, or attacking a porcupine only to get a muzzle full of quills.

In the afternoon he'd sit in the shade of the pool house with his iPad, reading articles and watching YouTube clips. If Matthew was around he'd try to interest him in whatever he was looking at. 'There's something authentic there,' was his typical opening comment, or 'That's the real thing, don't you think?' After which, having secured Matthew's agreement, he would come out with some deeper-level objection.

On one occasion he showed Matthew some video footage of the students on the Davis campus being pepper-sprayed by cops as they sat stoically on the ground, refusing to move.

'You can't question their authenticity,' he said, prodding his finger at the screen. 'I mean, you don't see that kind of courage without some authentic moral conviction underwriting it. Do you?'

Matthew made his usual murmur of assent.

'But what is it?' Charlie asked. 'What do they actually believe in? What do they even want? How come we don't remember what they were protesting or demanding? Did we ever in fact know?'

Sometimes in the early evening he'd sit in his meditation garden – a small, enclosed lawn with a stone Buddha at one end – or drive up to a sitting at the nearby Zen monastery, returning for dinner looking serene and smelling of sandalwood. Now and then he had to go into New York for meetings connected with the consultancy group he was trying to set up. He left early in the morning and it was understood that Chloe and Matthew would wait to eat until he got back, which was often not before eleven or midnight. Whatever the time, he'd want to talk and drink for a couple of hours before going to bed, and they'd sit with him on the terrace listening to his analysis of the day's meetings.

He seemed eager to discuss these meetings, whether they'd gone well or badly. It seemed to bolster his sense of their importance, and with that, his belief that he was making his way back into the game he'd been ousted from earlier that year. He'd never admitted to any feelings of rejection or failure after being 'let go' from his hedge fund, but Matthew knew him well enough to know it must have been a blow to his ego. Being without a recognised position in the world would have felt highly uncomfortable to him. There was nothing of the natural maverick or outsider about Charlie: he wasn't the type to base his self-esteem on his own judgement. He needed official recognition and approval. Whether that was a sign of virtue or weakness, Matthew wasn't sure, but he was certainly doing all he could to rebuild his career, and Matthew couldn't help comparing himself – bogged down in this peculiar inertia of his – unfavourably with his cousin, at least in this respect.

Chloe's routines were less predictable. Some days she did nothing but lie by the pool with a pile of magazines and her phone, ignoring both as she steeped herself in sunlight. She'd signed up for yoga and Zumba classes in town and some mornings she went off with her rolled-up mat and water canister, but often she didn't bother. Even when she did go off for a class she was capable of changing her mind, as Matthew discovered on one occasion when Charlie, who'd left his favourite tennis racquet in the Lexus, asked Matthew to grab it from the car on his way back from town, and the car had turned out not to be in the yoga studio parking lot.

She'd succumbed to her own laziness as she approached the studio, she confessed later, and spent her yoga hour in a café drinking a triple latte, from which she was still visibly sparkling with caffeinated good humour.

She did seem to be pursuing the mailbox idea, however, and would drift off with her cameras, usually in the late afternoon, to catch them at magic hour.

'That was such a good idea of yours, Matt,' she said, returning from one of these expeditions.

'Well, I can't wait to see the results.'

He thought of her driving around the country roads, making her judgements, setting up her cameras, filling her memory cards and rolls of film, all because he had casually suggested she might find these harmless things interesting, and this was as satisfying to him as if he had actually been driving around with her. The project had become another instance of that action-at-a-distance that his feelings for her thrived on, and that seemed to be all they required by way of sustenance.

As for his own routines, he took his role as chef seriously and spent much of his time driving around to farmers' markets or checking out little specialty stores hidden on rural roads or in the immigrant neighbourhoods of nearby towns. Whenever he set off he made a point of offering to do any errands that needed running. Charlie asked him to pick up some stones he'd ordered for an outdoor pizza oven he planned to build. One time Chloe asked him to get a copy of an entertainment magazine at the Barnes and Noble in East Deerfield. Occasionally she put in a request for kumquats and chocolate, her favourite snack. Otherwise it was mostly just dropping off dry-cleaning or taking the garbage to the town dump. A cleaning lady did their laundry at the house.

When he wasn't marketing he was usually swimming or sunbathing – mostly at the pool but sometimes at one of the swimming holes in the creek, the Millstream, that ran along the back of town. The clear, cold water fell into a series of pools defined by smooth-edged boulders that grew immensely warm by mid-morning. He would park the truck in the gravel lot by the bridge that connected the main part of town with some quieter residential roads. Stone steps led down under the bridge to the first of the pools and you could pick your way along the shelving stone banks to a half-dozen other pools running under the backyards of the private homes on the road that ran parallel with the creek. Trees at the top of the bank made it easy enough to find shade. He'd set up with a towel and his copy of Pascal or a magazine and watch the world go by.

There were packs of noisy high-schoolers, young couples staying in the nearby bed and breakfasts, elderly retirees with wrinkled white bodies. There was also a steady stream of Rainbow people and Dead-Heads who gravitated around Aurelia in the summer, camping in the woods behind the public meadow known locally as Paradise. On weekends they held late-night drumming sessions that you could hear all the way up at the house, and there were more low-key sessions, audible from the stream, that seemed to run pretty much continuously, adding their own frequency to that of the insects and birds, the pulsating dial tone of summer.

He found this latter group – the Rainbows and Dead-Heads – especially fascinating. They'd drift down to the water in the late afternoon in their beads and leather vests, trailing clouds of patchouli, often carrying their drums. Settling in groups on the smooth rocks, they'd preen and horse around with a mixture of childlike unselfconsciousness and highly self-conscious theatrical self-display.

He'd always had conflicting feelings about these hedonistic types. To live in that blaze of colour, scent and music, moving everywhere in loose tribal groups with everyone looking out for each other (at least in theory) appealed to a deep instinct in him. In his teens, after being expelled from school, he'd hung around on the fringes of an English version of the same subculture – travellers, hippies, 'freaks' as they called themselves. He had become, in a kind of perverse, retroactive justification for his expulsion, a small-scale dealer of pot and acid, and those were his customers. For a while he'd dreamed of leaving home, what remained of home, and becoming a fully fledged member of one or other of the groups. But something always held him back; some lingering attachment to respectability, but also a growing impatience with their constant petty criminality. These American counterparts struck him as more idealistic, or anyway less obviously out to rip each other off, though by this stage in his life he was too much himself to think, even jokingly, about joining them. But they interested him to observe.

One day a wizened old guy with grey hair in a red bandanna, who'd perched on the rocks next to Matthew and begun darning an embroidered shoulder bag, treated him to a rambling monologue about himself.

'I'm what we call an Early,' he said, taking Matthew's vague nod as an invitation to talk.

'An Early?'

'Early to the vision.'

He'd joined the Rainbow Family of Living Light in the early seventies, he told Matthew, right after the first 'Gathering of the Tribes', and had been 'dogging it' across country from gathering to gathering ever since. Now, he said, he was an official 'hipstorian' of the group.

'Designated vibeswatcher too,' he added with a gummy grin. 'And Shanti Sena. That's a peacekeeper.'

Matthew smiled back:

'I like the lingo!'

'Yep. See, when you quit Babylon you gotta make your own language for your own values. I'm saying, like Babylon talks about the *e*-conomy and the *e*-go, whereas we're all about the *we*-conomy and the *we*-go.'

'Nice.'

Two girls came by.

'Hey now, Pike,' they said.

'Hey now.'

They squatted down on the rock. One of them had pale green hair and a face like a kitten. The other had a lot of metal in her eyebrows and nose. They looked about eighteen. The air around them filled with a candy-like fragrance.

41

Pike (that seemed to be the old guy's name) told them that he and Matthew had been talking about the Family.

'I'm interested in it,' Matthew said encouragingly.

'Cool,' the one with the piercings said.

Her friend said: 'Fantastic.'

Both eyed Matthew warmly, as if excited to be sitting down with some obvious Babylonian.

'I'm explaining the lingo,' Pike said, chuckling softly. His thin old legs looked awfully hairy next to the smooth limbs of the girls in their very short cut-off jeans.

'You mean like Zuzus and Wahwahs?' the green-haired girl said.

'What are those?' Matthew asked.

'Different types of tasty morsels, you could say,' Pike offered.

'Drainbows,' the other girl offered. 'Hohners, Snifters.'

'All different types you find at the gatherings,' Pike put in.

'Heil Holies, Blissninnies.'

'Blissninnies!' Matthew repeated with a laugh. He was enjoying the little interlude, as much for its unexpectedness as anything else. He was about to ask the girls how they had come to join the Rainbows, when a tall, shirtless guy in a pair of ragged shorts walked barefoot slowly across their rock and the girls fell silent. He had long ringletted hair with gold glints in it, well-defined muscles and strong features that made Matthew think of Dürer's famous self-portrait. As he passed by, Matthew saw that he had **99%** inked on his left shoulder. He didn't say anything, but a few paces beyond their rock he turned around and, looking at the girls, made a laconic beckoning motion with one hand, turning again and continuing on his way: confident, apparently, that they would get up and follow him. They did.

Pike, glancing at Matthew, gave a sort of chuckle and busied himself with his darning.

It wasn't much of an incident, but it made an unpleasant impression on Matthew. He assumed the girls must have known the guy. But even so, that casually proprietorial gesture rankled with him. It seemed consciously insulting. The guy's physical appearance, which had struck Matthew as extremely calculated, also rankled. No shoes, no pack or bag, no clutter of any kind; as if he were proclaiming the utter self-sufficiency of the human animal, at least in his own fine case.

It occurred to Matthew that although he'd always been drawn to these types, he'd always been slightly irked by them too, regarding their rejection of 'Babylon' as a tacit admission that they lacked what it took to succeed there, but that unlike him, they refused to accept its judgement against them. So that for one of them to present himself as somehow, a priori, a superior being, was like a challenge that ought to have been answered.

'Who was that guy?' he asked.

Pike looked up from his bag.

'That's Torssen. He just showed up last week. We call him the Prince.'

'Why's that?'

'He likes to organise shit, I guess.'

'You mean he's political?'

'Yeah, kinda.'

'I noticed the tatt.'

'Right.'

'Is there much of a connection between you guys and Occupy?'

Pike knitted his brows.

'See, we're historically more a spiritual thing than a political thing. It's like, a different movie, dig? Our movie's not about protest so much as what do you give some kid who works minimum wage at a convenience store with no hope of getting out? They gotta have something to be *for*, not just against.'

Matthew nodded. He had detected a definite lack of enthusiasm on Pike's part for the 'Prince', and this endeared him to the old guy.

He smiled, suddenly amused at his own foolishness for letting something so trivial get to him. He went over the funny words in his mind, making an effort to commit them to memory. It would be something to talk about at dinner. Chloe would appreciate it. He could see that guileless involuntary smile of hers already in his mind's eye; feel in advance the appreciative brush of her hand on his arm.

Towards the middle of July the weather grew hotter, and with the heat came a muggy humidity that made it hard to be outside, even up on the mountain.

Chloe, when she wasn't out photographing or at one of her classes, sat in the living room with the A/C on high. Charlie also went out less. It was too hot for tennis and he spent most of his time working or meditating in the pool house, which was also air-conditioned.

Then the temperatures soared even higher, spiking into the high nineties.

The three of them sat in the living room one morning, playing Scrabble. Matthew's family had been avid Scrabble players and Charlie had been introduced to the game when he'd gone to live with them as a teenager. He hadn't much liked it – it hadn't accorded with his sense of what was 'cool': a novel concept in Matthew's old-fashioned home, but extremely important to the adolescent Charlie – and he hadn't been very good at it either. And yet as an adult he'd incorporated it into his own household rituals when Lily learned to read. The game seemed to have a significant emotional resonance for him, and Matthew was always touched when he suggested playing. It was as if his cousin were acknowledging the ancient bond between them.

Someone had managed 'SIOUX' and as a joke Matthew put a P at the end of it.

After a moment Chloe burst into laughter.

'I don't get it,' Charlie said.

Chloe explained:

'Soup. He's spelling soup.'

Matthew made to take the P away but Chloe said to leave it.

'It's hilarious.'

'Well, I'm not scoring the I or the X,' Charlie said.

'Don't be a spoilsport, Charlie,' Chloe told him quietly.

A frown crossed Charlie's face, but he said nothing.

After the game he left for New York where he had a late-afternoon meeting. A little later Chloe said she had to go out too.

'Anything interesting?' Matthew asked.

'Oh, I need to buy a present for Charlie,' she said vaguely, and then added, 'I've been feeling guilty about that T-shirt I bought him. It was so ungenerous compared with the bracelet he gave me. I want to get him something else.'

Matthew wished her luck. He had no idea what their financial arrangements were, but he assumed the money was all from Charlie's side and it amused him to think of Chloe feeling guilty about under-spending Charlie's money on a present for Charlie and then assuaging that guilt by spending more. At the same time he was touched, as always, by her quietly scrupulous devotion to her husband.

Later, lying on his bed in the guest house, he found himself thinking about the many different ways in which you can know a person, and the many kinds of knowledge that might not help you know them at all.

In Charlie's case, it seemed to him that the résumé more or less evoked the man. He was pretty sure that if he knew only that Charlie had become head prefect at the school they went to in London, had gone on to Dartmouth as a legacy student, had worked in banking and then hedge-fund management, was currently writing a screed on socially responsible investing, played tennis avidly, and practised some form of Zen Buddhism, the picture that would form in his mind would be pretty close to the actual Charlie he knew. But in Chloe's case nothing he ever learned about her in the biographical sense – that she'd grown up in suburban Indianapolis, the daughter of an engineer and a music teacher; that her boyfriend before Charlie had been a medical researcher for the World Health Organization; that she had once been one of Condé Nast's go-to photographers for fruits and berries – seemed to have any bearing at all on his actual knowledge of her.

She wasn't secretive exactly, but the essential elements of her nature did seem stowed in deep pockets hidden from public view – hidden even from each other, somehow.

Once, when he was up for a weekend visit, staying in the main house, he'd come down to an early breakfast to find her just returning from somewhere in the car. It turned out she'd been at Sunday Mass in East Deerfield. He'd had no idea she was religious, or for that matter that she was Catholic. Their daughter had been at the house that weekend but Chloe hadn't brought her along, which had seemed to further emphasise the very private nature of the thing.

Music too. He knew she was a discerning listener – early on they'd discovered a shared enthusiasm for the voice of Beth Gibbons; its strange vacillations between sweetness and caustic harshness. But Chloe turned out to be more than just a consumer of music. He'd happened to be passing their street in Cobble Hill one evening, just as Charlie was arriving home from work, and Charlie had invited him in for a drink. Piano music came from upstairs as they stepped in. A Beethoven sonata, he'd guessed, played by Ashkenazi or some other master of the Romantic. But the music stopped dead in the middle of a passage of complex glissandi, starting again a moment later, and he'd realised there was someone up there actually playing it. He'd asked Charlie who it was. 'Oh, that's Chlo,' he'd said, without great interest. 'She's good!' Matthew had exclaimed. Charlie had shrugged. 'I think she wanted to be a pro at some time but she wasn't quite up to it. She only plays now when there's no one around. Or when she thinks there isn't.'

And then, just a couple of days ago, Matthew had discovered another of these secret pockets of Chloe's personality.

It had been a baking, breezeless afternoon. The three of them had been lazing by the pool, when he saw that Chloe was looking closely at some of the flowering shrubs that ran along one side of the fence. Beyond enjoying the occasional scent of lavender wafting from them, Matthew hadn't taken any notice of these plant-ings. But as Chloe gazed steadily and purposefully along them, raising a pair of binoculars to her eyes from time to time even though the bed was only a few yards away, he'd started gazing at them too.

'What are you looking at?'

'The butterflies.'

48

Only then had he become conscious of the mass of wings in as many bright colours as the flowers themselves, trembling on the blossoms or hovering in the air above them.

It turned out Chloe had had the bed put in that spring and had selected the plantings specifically to attract butterflies. Handing Matthew the binoculars, she'd told him what the different plants were and which species each one attracted. Yellow Potentilla for the Coppers, Hackberry for the Checked Fritillaries, Purple Swamp Milkweed for the Monarchs. At this proximity the heavy Zeiss binoculars organised the space into a succession of flat, richly lit planes in which everything looked, paradoxically, more three-dimensional than it did to the naked eye. The effect was somewhat hallucinatory, and in fact, as he lost himself among the enormously magnified wings and velvety petals in which, alongside the butterflies, huge bumble bees with bulging gold bags of pollen at their thighs were cruising, Matthew remembered long summer afternoons in his teens when he would lie in the Kyoto Garden in Holland Park, tripping on Green Emeralds or some other species of acid left unsold from his morning jaunts down to the flyover at the bottom of the Portobello Road, and would seem to cross from his drab existence into some realm of fantastical enchantment.

That was Chloe; full of little surprises: pockets and recesses, inlets and oubliettes, with music in them, and Sunday Mass, and a garden full of butterflies.

Four

The temperature fell a little. It was still too hot to eat meat, but at dinner, after three days of chilled soups and composed salads, Charlie said he needed something to get his teeth into. The next morning Matthew called the fish counter at Morelli's to see what they had in fresh. It turned out they'd just had a delivery of line-caught striped bass from Nantucket.

'It'll go fast,' the man said.

Charlie and Chloe had gone off a few minutes earlier; Charlie in the convertible to an early sitting at the monastery, Chloe in the Lexus to her yoga class in Aurelia. Matthew had told them he was going to spend the morning by the pool, but when he found out about the bass he fired up the pickup and set off for East Deerfield, a half-hour drive.

The striped bass had been laid out on the counter when he got there. It looked superb, the flesh a gleaming alabaster white, the thin, stippled 'stripe' down its length a dark reddish colour as if a wounded bird had hopped across a field of snow. Nantucket striped bass fed on the sweet-fleshed baby squid that spawned off the eastern end of the island, rather than on mackerel or other oily creatures, which gave them an incomparably delicate flavour. Matthew bought two large slabs and for good measure some oysters and scallops, and had them packed in ice. Charlie had given him a credit card for buying provisions.

He was driving along the strip of gas stations and fast-food joints that led out of town when he saw a silver Lexus peel off to the right at the stop-light fifty yards ahead. As it climbed the steep access road to the mall, Chloe's head appeared in profile at the wheel. She'd changed out of the black tank top that she'd been wearing when she left the house, into a white blouse with short puffy sleeves, but it was definitely her.

He was confused, seeing her here in East Deerfield when she'd said she was going to her yoga class in Aurelia. He supposed she must have remembered some chore she had to do in East Deerfield. But even as he articulated the thought, he was aware that it didn't account for the change of clothing.

He was planning a stop at the mall himself to buy razors and toothpaste, and he kept his eye on the Lexus as he made the same turn. Actually, there was a whole complex of malls and big-box stores up there above the town, with parking lots around them and a labyrinth of branch roads looping in between.

At the top of the access road, where Lowe's and Walmart were signed off to the left, Chloe turned right, and although Matthew had planned to do his shopping at Walmart, he turned right also. Jumbled together in his mind as he made the turn were the thought that he could just as easily do his shopping at Target, which was in this direction, and the memory of a brief exchange he'd had with Chloe a few days ago when he'd asked if she'd found another anniversary present for Charlie and she hadn't seemed to know what he was talking about until he reminded her that she'd felt guilty about the T-shirt. 'Oh,' she'd said with a sort of brusque vagueness, 'no, I didn't find anything.' He'd dropped the subject but her obtuseness had seemed odd, and it came back to him now.

Keeping well behind, he followed Chloe past the sprawling, polygonal fortress that housed Target, Best Buy, Sears and Dick's Sporting Goods. He was just curious, was what he told himself, though he was aware of that not being entirely the truth. If he'd stopped to analyse himself more exactly, he would have realised that he was amusing himself with a kind of play-acting of husbandly suspicion. Beyond the Sears entrance, she branched off onto a subsidiary road that led back downhill past a Wendy's and around a hairpin bend. As Matthew rounded the bend, he saw that she'd turned off into the parking lot of a large, horseshoe-shaped building.

He drove on past, pulling into a laundromat a hundred yards further on, and doubling back. Driving slowly past the turn-off, he realised it was the rear entrance to the East Deerfield Inn, a motel you would normally access from the main road down below.

She was getting out of the Lexus as he passed. In place of the yoga pants she'd been wearing when she left the house, she had on a summer skirt. She must have changed her clothing on the way here, he thought, glimpsing her in his mirror. She'd known in advance she was coming, which meant that the business about going to yoga was a premeditated lie.

The play-acting sensation had worn off by now, giving way to the less amusing knowledge that he was in fact spying on her. He considered going home and forcing himself not to think about it. But he doubted whether that would be possible, and anyway it occurred to him that, however distasteful it might be, he was under an obligation of friendship to stick around. A double obligation, in fact: one to Chloe in case her presence here turned out to have an innocent explanation, and one to Charlie in case it didn't.

He had an idea that he might be able to see down into the motel court from the Wendy's parking lot on the road above it, beyond the hairpin turn, but when he got there he saw that there was a guard rail around the lot that made it impossible to get close enough to the embankment. All he could see was a slice of the building's flat roof with its bric-a-brac of vents and turban-like fans.

He had no choice but to get out of the truck. Assuming the confident air of someone on legitimate business, he climbed over the guard rail. A stand of thin trees beyond it led to the edge of the embankment, which fell away steeply, giving a view into the motel parking lot. The ground under the trees was littered with old wrappings of burgers and fries. Truck-sized blocks of yellowish stone formed a retaining wall at the bottom of the slope.

Chloe was walking across the parking lot, carrying a canvas bag. Reaching a door on the left arm of the building, with some kind of vintage maroon car parked outside it, she knocked once. The door opened, and she stepped inside.

The day was already stifling. Even in the shade of the little trees where Matthew was standing, it was intensely hot. He stared at the distant door, not knowing what else to do. From time to time he looked briefly away, as if to rest his eyes from a glare.

Twenty minutes passed; half an hour. As the sun climbed higher in the sky the saplings gave less shade. Beads of sweat began trickling down Matthew's face and neck and under his shirt. He stood there, motionless. It seemed to him he had a responsibility to remain in sight of the door. At the same time, however, he couldn't bear to think what might be going on behind it, so that even as he studiously faced out in that direction, his mind was just as studiously avoiding it.

A few crickets, day-shift replacements for the katydids that chorused at night, chirped in the foliage. Traffic exhaust mingled with fumes of hot grease. He heard a couple of people pause behind him as they crossed the parking lot. He didn't turn and they continued on their way. He was barely sheltered now from the mid-morning blaze.

Almost an hour had passed by the time the door opened and Chloe came out. Her hair looked damp. She was wearing her yoga pants again, and the black tank top. The sandals were back on too. She climbed into the Lexus, and Matthew watched her drive away.

He turned to leave, but then changed his mind. What if there really was an innocent explanation for the visit? He tried to come up with a possible scenario. Nothing he could think of seemed terribly likely, but if anyone was capable of secretly pursuing some unexpected but completely benign activity, it was Chloe.

After about fifteen minutes the door opened again and a man came out, carrying a leather duffel bag. He had a wide head, framed in collar-length hair, and a triangle of pointed beard. A stout, if firm-looking, belly swelled under his billowing blue shirt. Sturdy knees and stocky calves narrowed from his cargo shorts into a pair of blue deck shoes.

He unlocked the maroon car, threw in his bag, and drove away.

Matthew turned and climbed back over the guard rail. He felt as though he had been briefly concussed. Spots drifted on his vision; nausea swayed in his stomach.

Opening the door of the pickup he was hit with a blast of fishy-smelling heat. In his rush earlier, he'd neglected to leave a window open and now the fish was half-cooked. He threw it out and went back to Morelli's, where the same man served him the same quantities of striped bass and shellfish as he had ordered before. From the man's sly expression, he seemed to imagine Matthew had absent-mindedly forgotten that he'd already made this exact purchase an hour and a half earlier.

*   *   *

56

Charlie was at the house when he got back, excavating a Brillat-Savarin cheese he'd brought from the city on his last visit. He had a weakness for pungent cheeses and a habit of gorging on them in private, scooping out the soft centres and leaving the hollowed rind.

'No tennis?' Matthew asked, putting the Morelli's bag in the fridge. He was so uncomfortable he could barely bring himself to look at his cousin. His intention, to the extent that he'd formed one, had been to tell Charlie everything he'd seen at the motel, as soon as he could find a suitable moment. It was just an emergency response at this stage, not a considered plan. The urge to rid himself of the incident, obliterate it from his mind, was overwhelming, and telling Charlie seemed the best hope of accomplishing this.

Charlie yawned.

'Too hot.'

Chloe's car crunched on the gravel outside a few minutes later – she must have been killing time so as not to be home from 'yoga' too early – and she came into the kitchen, smiling absently and waggling her fingers as she passed through into the sunken living room, where she collapsed in one of the sofas with a copy of the *Aurelia Gazette*.

She'd made the same kind of entrance numerous times and there hadn't seemed anything remarkable about it. It was just a natural way of observing basic courtesies while asserting her wish to remain in her own private space. But now it seemed to Matthew steeped in guile.

'How was yoga?' he asked.

She didn't seem to hear the question.

'Chlo – Matt's asking how yoga was,' Charlie said.

'Oh, sorry, Matt. It was great, thanks.'

She flashed him her lovely smile and resumed her reading.

He had to admire her poise, but to have betrayed that smile of hers, which had always seemed to him the ultimate expression of her intense and innocent capacity for joy; to have sent that smile out on a mission so perfidious, was strangely upsetting.

Into his mind came another memory: the time her car hadn't been in the yoga parking lot when Charlie had asked him to get his tennis racquet, and she'd claimed to have been in some café instead, drinking a triple latte. He saw her again in his mind's eye as she recounted it, making fun of her own enervated laziness with the same sparkling smile as she wore now, and the treachery seemed to spread like a crack into the past.

In the afternoon Charlie went out on some errand and Chloe disappeared upstairs. When Charlie came back he went up to join her, and the two of them stayed up there the rest of the day.

Matthew lay by the pool, watching the butterflies. Fu yelped periodically, wanting his walk, but Matthew was damned if he was going to offer to take him. He was going over the events of the morning, retracing the sequence from the moment he'd spotted Chloe ahead of him on the road below the mall, to her exit from the motel, and the man's emergence a little later. The discomfort provoked by the memory of the events was as sharp as it had been during their actual occurrence, and he wished he could think about something else – his own problems, for instance; the question of how to get himself out of his rut, jumpstart his career, find a less grim apartment – which were after all the things he'd come up here to address – but it appeared to be impossible. Again in his mind the events revolved: Chloe at the wheel in her white blouse; the blunt little jolt inside him as he'd realised something suspicious was going on; the hot vigil at the edge of the Wendy's parking lot; Chloe in her summer skirt entering the motel . . . It seemed to him he had been presented with some difficult problem to which he alone could provide the solution, and which he was under an obligation to solve as quickly as possible. But instead of formulating an answer, or even groping in the direction of an answer, his mind simply repeated the little sequence yet again, so that once more he was turning up onto the access road behind Chloe, following her past Target and Dick's Sporting Goods, climbing over the curved metal guard rail, and standing motionless under the thin trees staring at the motel door with its glinting handle, while the fume-filled air grew hotter and hotter.

Around six, he started on the dinner. He'd intended to cook a version of a Catalan seafood dish that matches a firm, white fish with a mixture of blood sausage and sea urchin roe, seasoned with chorizo. He had some decent chorizo from Fairway and he'd bought some Morcilla blood sausage at the place near Poughkeepsie. It wasn't the same as Catalan *botifarra negra* which tended to be lighter on the cloves and cinnamon, but it was the only type you could get in the States and it gave the palate the same kind of womby, cave-like background from which to fall on the sweet flesh of the bass. In place of the sea urchin roe he planned to butter-fry the oysters and scallops.

Charlie and Chloe usually drifted into the kitchen for a drink well before dinner, but they were still upstairs by the time everything was ready. Once or twice during previous visits, Matthew had heard discreet sounds of lovemaking come down through the ceiling, and he'd been vaguely listening out for them, but he hadn't heard anything, and he supposed that was less disturbing than it would have been if he had, all things considered, though it didn't do much to alleviate the tension inside him. The thought of telling Charlie what he'd seen that morning, while still presenting itself as his only option, had been filling him with dread. He'd have to find some way of doing it as soon as possible; preferably tonight. He didn't want it lingering over him.

He called up but there was no reply. Feeling awkward, he went to the bottom of the stairs and called again. After a while Charlie answered groggily 'Yeah?' and Matthew told him dinner was ready.

They both made an effort to be sociable when they finally came down, but he could tell they hadn't wanted to be disturbed, and that neither of them much wanted to eat. They sat out on the terrace with the usual candlelight and katydid chorus, but it was a lacklustre affair. Charlie explained apologetically that he'd eaten too much cheese earlier, and barely picked at his food. Chloe at least made an effort but she was obviously distracted by her own thoughts.

'How's Lily getting on at camp?' Matthew asked her.

She gave some vague answer, and he felt a bit malicious for raising the subject. Soon afterwards she stood up and asked if they'd mind if she went to bed.

'Everything okay?' Charlie said.

'Yes. I'm just tired.'

She yawned and waved goodnight.

'Another delicious dinner, Matt. Thank you.'

'You're welcome,' he said, pleasure rising in him, in spite of himself.

Alone with Charlie, he decided he might as well get the unpleasant task over. He was racking his brains to think of some appropriate way to introduce the subject, when Charlie gave a loud yawn and said that he also was feeling tired.

'Would you mind if I hit the hay?'

'Of course not,' Matthew said, relieved.

The bulk of summer still lay ahead of him, he reflected later, in bed. All year he'd been looking forward to the long hot weeks up here. He needed them badly. He'd been counting on them to restore him, bring him out of the strange funk he'd drifted into. Was he really going to have to spoil these precious days? Because one way or another that would surely be the effect if he spilled the beans on Chloe. He hadn't thought it through earlier, but now that he did he could see that telling Charlie was going to wreck the summer – for all three of them.

But how the hell could he *not* tell Charlie? Wasn't he obliged to? Obviously it would be easier not to; just to go on as if nothing had happened, but the very fact that it *would* be easier, seemed to confirm that what he needed to do was precisely the difficult thing. Wasn't that his responsibility as Charlie's cousin and friend? And would it be possible, anyway, to salvage the summer by pretending nothing had happened?

Briefly, as he posed these questions he became aware of something minutely false in presenting the problem to himself in terms of friendship and cousinly duty: a sheen of spuriousness overlaying the formula. It wasn't how he'd seen it this morning, after all, but somehow an emergency measure, conceived purely to expunge the intolerable reality from his own mind, had morphed into something more altruistic, a 'duty', and he didn't trust altruism, or not when it fronted his own impulses. His mind stalled, overcome by the complexity of the situation. On top of the question of whether or not to tell Charlie, there was the question – possibly even more unsettling – of how this new knowledge was going to affect his own relationship with Chloe; a whole dense layer of potential damage that he hadn't yet been able to bring himself to inspect.

He thought of Charlie over at the Zendo that morning; pictured him in the lotus position, pinched fingers on his sunburned knees: being 'in the moment' while Chloe was doing whatever she'd been doing back in that motel room . . . . It occurred to him that *he* had actually been the one in Charlie's 'moment', and that, far from being a state of bliss, it had been extremely painful.

It was somewhat typical of Charlie, he found himself thinking, to arrange for someone else to feel his pain.

Five

Several days passed. The same routines filled them as before. But their regularity no longer had the same agreeably lulling effect on Matthew. When Chloe set off to take pictures or attend one of her classes, it was impossible to avoid the question of whether she was in fact going off to meet the man from the motel, and the thought would leave him jangling with useless emotions. Meanwhile the sight of Charlie working or meditating, or driving off in his tennis gear, formed an image of increasingly irritating innocence. Even his own pleasantly mindless activities were losing their charm, their soothing rhythms broken by gusts of crackling interference from a situation that had nothing to do with the problems he was trying to sort out.

But what was he supposed to do? The feeling that he ought to tell Charlie about the motel remained undiminished despite recurrences of that sense of something false about it, or at least something glossed over. Yet he was finding it vastly more difficult to tell Charlie than he had foreseen. Whenever he tried, a curious, contradictory impulse would take over. Cornering Charlie in his meditation garden or down in the wine cellar, he would begin by steering the conversation to the closeness and longevity of their friendship, meaning to prepare Charlie for the necessary blow. But within moments another part of his mind would send out torrents of diversionary chatter; meaningless blather about his own life and plans – the food truck idea, or his hope of being able to afford a bigger apartment before long, or any other topic besides the one he'd intended to raise. Charlie would look at him strangely at these moments, and Matthew knew he risked appearing a little crazy, but it was always a relief to come away from him with the secret intact, the blow still undelivered.

Who wants to be the bearer of such tidings? If Charlie believed him he'd be devastated. If he didn't – and that was obviously a possibility – he would think Matthew was deliberately stirring up trouble. Either way he would almost certainly resent him. And it wasn't just the summer that stood to be ruined as a result, but their whole, precariously reconstructed friendship, which for all its stresses and imbalances had become as important to Matthew this time around as it had been the first time.

So he prevaricated: told himself he needed more evidence before doing something so potentially destructive; that he'd perhaps misconstrued the episode at the motel; that Chloe and the man might have been transacting some perfectly legitimate business in his room; that even the seemingly undeniable element of deception – claiming she was going to yoga, changing her clothes – had some innocent explanation. He tried to convince himself that even if he found rock-solid evidence of an affair, his duty was actually to protect Charlie rather than inflict pain on him. Or else that it was to find some way of quietly bringing the affair to an end: confronting Chloe, dropping a hint, or just somehow making her feel he was watching her . . . All of which seemed to him equally impossible and repugnant.

What he settled on, in the end, was the formula that it was simply none of his business. *None of my business*, he would tell himself firmly as Chloe left the house, and the agitation started up in his heart. *None of my business*, as the unruffled contentment of Charlie's demeanour prompted that sudden sharp urge to shatter it. *None of my business* . . . And after a while a fragile calm would descend on him.

One morning he was at the Greenmarket in Aurelia, waiting to pay, when he became aware of a presence at the next register. Before even turning he caught a familiar signal on his antennae. A direct glance confirmed it. There was the beefily built figure, the Van Dyke beard, the grey-streaked dark hair falling in wiry clusters either side of the broad, sharp-tipped chin. The untucked shirt, pink this time, was worn in the same billowing style, over knee-length breeches. It was the man from the motel.

He stared, unable to stop himself.

The man looked solidly in his forties; hale and undimmed, but with no trace of the youthful uncertainty men in their thirties still project. His blocky nose jutted. His eyes were small but lively, glancing around the store with a ready-to-be-entertained look. It didn't surprise Matthew to hear him comment on what a gorgeous day it was to the sales clerk when his turn at the register came. What did come as a surprise was the accent: it was the self-delighting twang of a Southerner used to being found charming in the North. As his purchases crossed the scanner, Matthew observed them closely, and with growing consternation: bread, milk, coffee, olive oil, eggs, sea salt – not the purchases of someone staying in a motel. A bag of kumquats and some bars of chocolate appeared; still more disconcerting.

'Paper or plastic?' the clerk asked.

'Oh, I think I'll take the paper, miss. A day like this makes you want to save the planet, dudn' it?'

He left, carrying the bag against his stomach. Matthew, who was still waiting in line, considered jettisoning his own shopping so as to drive after him, but resisted, not wanting to draw attention to himself.

As it happened the man was walking, not driving. Leaving the store, Matthew saw him at the upper exit of the parking lot. Matthew put his own shopping into the truck, and walked after him, keeping well back. After crossing Tailor Street the man cut through a passageway next to the hardware store into a quiet back alley that led past a communal vegetable garden to the bridge across the Millstream creek. Matthew followed him over the bridge, where he turned left along Veery Road, the street that ran parallel with the creek. It was a residential street of houses in large private yards with tall hedges and fruit trees and rustic split-rail fences. There was no sidewalk. The houses on the left backed onto the high bank of the creek, and it was into the driveway of one of these – a simple whitewashed A-frame with a screened-in porch – that the man now entered. He was lifting the domed black lid off a Weber grill with his free hand as Matthew reached the driveway. The same hand a moment later stuck a key in the front door of the A-frame, opening it. The maroon vintage car Matthew had seen outside the motel was parked in the driveway. It was a Chrysler LeBaron.

Matthew walked on to the end of the road which eventually curved around to intersect with the County Road, and made a left onto Tailor Street. From there he crossed to the Greenmarket parking lot and climbed back into his truck.

So, he was here. Not ten miles away in an East Deerfield motel this time, but right here in Aurelia. Staying here, it appeared; renting or borrowing that A-frame. Buying supplies for himself. Stocking up (the thought sent its own painful reverberation through Matthew) on Chloe's favourite snack.

All of which implied what, exactly? Was there any difference between a lover who lived far away and had to rent a motel room to visit, and a lover who moved right in under the husband's nose? No. Infidelity was infidelity.

But as he drove back up the mountain he felt the encroachment of new disturbances. He found himself

67

imagining the progression of feelings between the two lovers that must have taken place in order to bring about this development: tender exchanges about missing each other; increasingly bold proposals for how to be together more often. It seemed to him he could hear, almost as if it were taking place right there in the car, the conversation the lovers must have had, breathless with the thrill of illicit passion – *I want to be with you all the time . . . I want that too . . . What if I had a place of my own up here . . .? What if I found you somewhere in the listings . . .?* None of his business, he repeated mechanically to himself, and yet it seemed to him he could feel, on his own senses, the mounting excitement at the new intensities of passion, intimacy, danger, that such a move would bring about. And by the time he got back to the house there was no doubt in his mind that things had taken a serious turn for the worse.

The next day at breakfast, Chloe asked Charlie what he was planning to do that morning.

'I have a conference call. Why?'

'There's a preview for an estate sale at one of those mansions across the river. I thought you might want to help me pick out some things.'

'Sorry, Chlo. I have the call scheduled. I did tell you about it.'

'Did you? I forgot. Anyway, it doesn't matter. The preview's on all week.' She yawned. 'I think I'll go to yoga in that case.'

She cleared a few things off the table and called goodbye from the kitchen.

'Are you coming right back?' Charlie asked.

'Yes?'

'Grab me a watermelon juice, would you?'

'Sure.'

She left in the Lexus. The sense of something catastrophic arising inside him gripped Matthew. Some explosive force seemed to be coming at him from within. He stood up, staggering a little as he pushed back the chair. Charlie glanced up from his iPod.

'You okay?'

'Yeah. I'm actually going to head off too. Do the shopping before it gets too hot.'

'All right, Matt.'

He drove straight to the Yoga Center, a barn-like wooden building down a cul-de-sac at the back of town. The Lexus wasn't in the parking lot. He'd predicted it wouldn't be, and yet its absence genuinely shocked him. He couldn't quite connect Chloe with the blatantness of her lie.

He drove straight to Veery Road, slowing as he approached the short driveway to the A-frame. The LeBaron was in the driveway, but not the Lexus. But the comfort its absence afforded was short-lived: he found the car less than a hundred yards away, hidden behind a small commercial strip with office buildings and a wine store, where Veery Road intersected with the County Road leading out of town. Evidently Chloe had decided it wasn't safe to park right in her lover's driveway.

Well, and so what to do? The explosive feeling had passed, leaving a kind of murkily ruminant confusion.

In a dim way he'd assumed that the possession of unequivocal knowledge would spur him into some equally unequivocal action. But in fact he felt less clear than ever. The idea of going back to the house and telling Charlie he could catch his wife in flagrante if he hurried down to Veery Road, was too grotesque to countenance. But to go back and say nothing, seemed just as awful. Telling himself he needed to think, he circled back through town and went down to the creek, leaving the truck in the parking lot by the bridge.

The rocks near the bridge were crowded with the usual idlers and vacationers. Downstream the numbers thinned out. He spotted a promising ledge on the other side of the creek. The fast-flowing water was too wide to jump, and he rolled up the legs of his pants to cross. From the rock, looking downstream, he saw the blue-trimmed white apex of the A-frame, standing out above hedges on the other side. If he walked another fifty yards and climbed up the steep bank, he would be standing in its backyard.

Had he come here in order to do that? He hadn't been conscious of it, but what other reason would there have been to come? And yet what could possibly be gained by placing himself there?

What do I want? he wondered. What am I looking for? Did he need to see Chloe in the house, with the man, in order to satisfy himself that his appraisal of the situation was correct? Surely that wasn't necessary. What then? Baffled by his own actions, he climbed off the rock and walked back upstream.

A group of Rainbows was settling in on a flat reddish slab where the water fell in combs from one level to another. At their centre, unmistakable with his Dürer ringlets and the cobble-like muscles of his arms and torso, was Mr 99%. Torssen. The 'Prince'. He had a baguette in his hands and was breaking off pieces to share out. He was laughing, his teeth gleaming in the morning sun, and the others were laughing too, their silver- and leather-bangled arms stretched out towards him. Some of them were pretending to plead for their morsel of bread like children, adding further to that sense they always gave off as a group, of staging and performing their own busy merriment for the benefit of others: the Babylonians presumably, whom of course they affected at the same time not to notice. It was striking, but even more so was the almost – no, it had to be fully – conscious manner in which this charismatic breaker of bread was reproducing in his own gestures those of Christ from a thousand illustrations of the miracle of the Loaves and Fishes. You had to hand it to the guy, Matthew thought; he had a gift for striking a pose. His long, sinewy arms made their motion of breaking and offering the glazed loaf (it looked like one of the over-aerated 'French sticks' that the local bakery, Early-to-Bread, sold) with an ease and grace that seemed to source the action in some utterly natural impulse of generosity.

Matthew passed on, wondering why he felt so irritated by these harmless people, and so ill-disposed towards the ringletted man in particular.

When he drove back behind the wine store the Lexus was gone. He looked at his watch: an hour had passed since the beginning of Chloe's 'yoga'. She'd be on her way home, he realised; with Charlie's juice. Watermelon juice! Cynical amusement brought a smile to his lips as he thought of the thin, astringent flavour of this decoction that Charlie was so fond of. It seemed a fitting gift, somehow, from his unfaithful wife.

He was such a funny mixture of weakness and strength, Charlie. Or softness and hardness. He could be ruthless, that was for sure; selfish in the extreme. But there was that hurt, vulnerable side to him too. Whenever Matthew found himself thinking too harshly of him, he would remind himself of this.

He remembered an incident from the evenings he and Charlie had shared when Matthew first came to the States. They'd been in one of the Bottle Service clubs on 27th Street that Charlie had frequented for a brief period, where he would pay five hundred dollars for a bottle of vodka and, when he was drunk enough, invite women to their table. They'd just sat down, when a silver-haired man had come over to say hello to Charlie. Charlie had seemed guarded, and when the man left, he'd downed his drink in a single gulp, baring his teeth at the burn.

'Have you ever been fucked in the ass?' he'd asked. 'Because that's what that guy did to me.' The incident he'd recounted to Matthew had occurred when Charlie was working as an analyst. The bank had been doing an IPO for a telecom equipment company, and the silver-haired man – a senior manager – had been pressing

Charlie to join him on a junket in Las Vegas, where the company was giving a presentation to potential investors. Analysts weren't supposed to go near these presentations, and Charlie had asked his boss to shield him from the improper pressure coming from the silver-haired guy. But instead of shielding him, the boss had made it clear that Charlie would lose a chunk of his bonus if he didn't go. It wasn't the bonus itself that he cared about, Charlie had said, but the year-end review. If that was bad, as it would be if he held out, he'd be finished in the business. So he'd gone to Vegas, accepted the courtesy suite at the Bellagio, the limitless Pol Roget champagne, the hospitality bag stuffed full of Hermès ties and Zegna cufflinks, and in return had written a report that smoothed over the company's liquidity problems and minimised the threats to its long-term market share posed by its rivals, and in short had let himself, as he repeated with morbid self-disgust, be 'royally fucked in the ass'.

He'd never mentioned the episode again, and Matthew had forgotten it until now. It must have been the humiliation Charlie was undergoing at the moment, albeit unwittingly this time, that had brought it back.

Six

In the period that followed, Matthew found himself heading off into town several times a day on some pretext or other – invented as much for his own benefit as anyone else's – and driving around in the vague hope (or was it dread? – he wasn't quite sure), of glimpsing Chloe's lover.

It seemed important to get some sense of the guy: some idea, as he put it to himself, of what he was 'up against'. There was also the fact that being in motion like this offered the sensation of doing something about the problem without committing him to the irreversible course of actually breaking the news to Charlie. At a certain level of consciousness he was aware of something unnecessary, and possibly even a little unhealthy, in what he was doing. What difference could it make, after all, even if he did pick up some nugget of information about the guy? And yet that awareness was peculiarly thin and ineffectual. Indulging in these meandering little expeditions seemed to satisfy some sharp craving in him. He almost felt as if he were at work, in some obscure way, on the recalcitrant stuff of his *own* existence.

He would cruise slowly past the A-frame, and if the LeBaron wasn't there, would look through the parking lots around town in search of its distinctive boxy maroon outline. He saw it outside the Fedex office on one occasion, in the Millstream Inn's parking lot on another. Twice, he saw the man himself in the Greenmarket. The second time he followed him from there to the movie rental store next door and stood behind him as he returned a DVD. His neck was tanned reddish at the back. He wore a beige canvas cap from which his hair bunched out in wiry curls. Dark stains showed at the armpits of his faded blue T-shirt, the sweat smell partly masked by a coriander-scented deodorant. He wasn't obviously good-looking in the way Charlie was, but he had a certain dynamism about him, Matthew had to admit; an unrefined if not quite crude forcefulness even when he stood still, that reminded Matthew of a statue he'd seen on his trip to Europe with his father, of some artistic colossus portrayed stark naked, with a jovial grin. His calf muscles, big as hams, were palely furred below his cargo shorts. He engaged the clerk in friendly conversation, his voice quiet but commanding, with a pleasant buzzing edge. 'It's a great little movie, you should see it,' he told her, exiting the store.

Matthew watched him cross the parking lot back to his car, before leaving the place himself. What had he learned? In terms of hard information, nothing. Yet for some reason he drove away with a sense of having

76

accomplished something, and for the rest of the afternoon he found himself reliving the little sequence: following the man once again in his mind's eye from the Greenmarket to the rental place, standing behind him at the register, watching him return the movie. The memory of the statue he'd seen became clearer in his mind. It seemed to superimpose itself on his image of the man, supplanting his features and figure with its own more archetypal embodiment of stout-bellied vigour, striding the earth with jovially arrogant confidence. Was that how Chloe saw him? It seemed to him, in that close proximity he often felt to the current of Chloe's feelings, that it was, and that for precisely this reason it absolved her, at least in her own mind, of hypocrisy. She had her own code of conduct: he'd always sensed that. For all her churchgoing sweetness and compassion, what motivated her wasn't the ambition to be a 'good person' in any conventional sense (Charlie was the conventional one in that respect), but simply a desire to engage with whatever offered the promise of life, energy, vitality. It was, he realised with a sort of gloomy clarity, one of the things he most admired about her.

A few days later, after he'd been puttering around town for the better part of the morning, he caught sight of the man again, approaching on foot from the far end of Veery Road. He continued driving towards him, aware of the black hemlocks and green laurel hedges flowing backwards around him as the distance closed between them. He'd been mentally planning a dinner of scallops and pork belly with a parmesan *espuma* as he drove around, and had realised he'd forgotten to bring any spare cartridges for his foamer when the man's stocky figure had appeared in the distance. He was walking on Matthew's side of the road, sensibly facing the oncoming traffic, and carrying a shiny white shopping bag with a bottle in it: champagne, Matthew saw as he drew closer and the foil top glittered. He found himself simultaneously wondering where he might be able to get hold of nitrous oxide cartridges for the *espuma*, picturing the man pouring a foaming glass of champagne for Chloe as they lay in bed, and realising with a sudden gush of aggression that with nothing more than a quick jerk of the steering wheel he could knock him down, run right over his thick neck, and be gone before anyone knew what had happened.

Instead, he slowed down politely and swung wide of him, receiving an appreciative nod in return.

He felt shaken after that. He hadn't realised he bore the guy actual hostility. The 'incident', purely imaginary as it had been, made him aware he was getting a little overwrought about the whole business.

It seemed to him he had been given a warning: to pull back, or at least formulate a more rational, practical plan of action than this rather aimless toing and froing.

But a plan to do what, exactly? Aside from the desire for things to be restored to their original condition, which was hardly a realistic aim, he had no clear objective around which to build a plan.

*　*　*

That afternoon Chloe announced she was going out to photograph some more mailboxes. There was one in particular, she said, that would make a good cover for a book if she ever collected them.

'Where's that?' Matthew asked, adding quickly, so as to cover the tone of suspicion he'd caught in his own voice: 'I mean, I was wondering if I'd seen it.'

She smiled, gathering up her car keys.

'Probably not. It's on a road that doesn't really lead anywhere.'

Charlie, who was on his iPad at the kitchen table and hadn't seemed to be following the conversation, said, without looking up:

'Which road?'

'Fletcher,' Chloe answered without hesitation. 'Just past the place that sells ducks' eggs. Why don't you come with me and take a look? It's very pretty. You too, Matthew, if you'd like . . .'

Charlie grunted: 'Maybe another time,' and Matthew, realising he'd been outmanoeuvred, muttered that he was a little tired.

'Well, come down later if you feel like it,' Chloe said, smiling at each of them. 'I'll be there till sunset.'

As she left, Matthew saw Charlie glancing after her, and thought he caught something uneasy in his expression. He had in fact considered the possibility that Charlie had some inkling of what was going on. He happened to know that his cousin had a problem with jealousy. In those candid talks they'd had during the first months of their reunion in New York, when Charlie was still hurting

79

from the break-up of his first marriage and glad of a willing listener, he'd confided in Matthew that one of the reasons for the break-up was that he'd driven Nikki, his wife, crazy with his suspicions. He'd wanted a kid, and when she'd said she wasn't ready he'd taken that – by his own shamefaced admission – as evidence that she wanted to go on, in his words, 'fooling around with other guys'. He'd changed since then, obviously. Under Chloe's steadying influence the anguished, self-flagellating Charlie of those days had given way to the contented husband and father that now formed the image he presented to the world, and presumably he'd learned to ignore the tremors of his hyper-vigilant instincts. But those instincts were surely still alive in him somewhere, however much he might wish to suppress what they were telling him. And if that were the case, might he not, at some level, be actually grateful for an opportunity to talk?

True, he'd shown no sign of interest in Matthew's attempts so far to open the subject, but then those attempts had been so indirect that it was entirely possible Charlie hadn't even realised what they were.

All of which seemed to argue for a more direct approach, or at least (caution intervening once again as the decision formed to broach the topic) a less oblique one.

'You seem,' Matthew said, perching on a kitchen stool, 'really happy, you and Chloe.'

Charlie looked up at him.

'I'd say we're pretty happy.'

'You seem to have a great balance between together-ness and . . . independence.'

'Uh-huh.'

'I admire that.'

'Well, Chloe's always been totally her own person.'

'I know.'

Charlie continued looking at him, as if his curiosity had been piqued, and Matthew felt he could safely develop the point.

'Unusually so, I'd say, compared with what I've noticed in other married couples.'

Charlie seemed to mull this over.

'What do you mean?'

'Oh, just that she seems to have these very strongly demarcated areas of her life that she keeps . . . private.'

'Such as?'

'I suppose I'm thinking of the way she goes off for her classes, or the photography. I mean, I think it's good to have that kind of separation in a relationship. I think it's a real strength.'

'It seems pretty normal to me.'

'Absolutely. Absolutely.'

Now he was afraid he'd misjudged Charlie's mood after all, or else scared him off.

'I guess I'm comparing it to the way you described your relationship with Nikki.'

Charlie's jaw-muscle clenched a moment.

'Yeah, well, it's definitely very different from that.'

'You used to get suspicious whenever she went out alone, right?'

'I was an idiot.'

'Though you did always, I mean . . .'

Matthew faltered, sensing danger.

'I did what?'

'Well, you did always maintain that your suspicions were probably justified . . .'

A frown crossed Charlie's features. He was silent for a moment.

'I've evolved since then,' he said, finally. 'I think it's important to take responsibility for your own character defects. I've tried to.'

He looked at his watch.

'Listen, Matt, I'm thinking I might head up to Hudson. There's a burgundy tasting I sort of want to go to.'

'That sounds fun.'

Charlie stood up. 'Well . . . You're welcome to join me.'

Matthew hesitated; a car ride together might be just the thing to force him to bring this distasteful business to an end. He glanced back over at Charlie, intending to accept the invitation, but was stalled by an expression in Charlie's eyes. They seemed to be regarding him with an odd neutrality.

'I mean, it's kind of an invitation thing', Charlie said, looking away. 'But I'm sure it'll be fine if you come along as my guest.'

Reflexively, though with a dim sense of being a little cowardly, Matthew grasped at the excuse to delay action once again.

'Oh. Thanks. Actually, maybe I'll stay here. Work on my tan . . .'

Charlie nodded.

'I'll see you later then.'

He left, grabbing his keys from the countertop.

Matthew sat down at the table where Charlie had been. It struck him that it might have been tactless to mention Nikki. Not that he'd had any reason to suspect Charlie was still sore about his ex after all these years, but he did know it was a mistake to underestimate Charlie's sensitivity in general. Stupid of me, he thought. Next time he'd go straight to the point. Say what he'd seen at the mall and let Charlie take it or leave it. No more beating about the bush.

It was five o'clock. He stood up, wondering what to do with himself. Two or three hours of solitude lay ahead of him. It should have been an appealing prospect, but it was filling him with curious apprehensiveness, as if the blank stretch of time were mined with strange perils. It seemed to him, oddly, that he was capable of doing something he might regret if he were not careful, though he couldn't imagine what form any such action might take. He considered his options.

Really he ought to get started on the project of taking stock of himself that he'd managed to avoid so far. He could have a swim, a skinny dip even, since he had the pool to himself, and then lie in a deckchair and do some good hard thinking.

It occurred to him that, for that matter, he had the whole house to himself. He was standing by the staircase now, a flight of polished planks that seemed held in their curving succession by pure air. He'd had no occasion to go up them on this visit, but there was no particular sense that the upstairs was off-limits. He began climbing.

The air up there was different: warmer, sweeter, redolent of soaps and lotions and Chloe's scent rather than the cooking smells and faint rawhide odour that permeated the downstairs spaces.

He didn't have anything specific in mind. 'I'll see if they've done anything different to the spare room,' he said to himself, opening the first door. The blond-wood sleigh bed still dominated the room but there was a new dresser next to it: deco, he guessed from its simple lines. Some fifties-looking ceramic vases had been arranged along the windowsill. Not that interesting, he thought, articulating the words as if to supply himself with some kind of harmless official motivation for moving on along the corridor.

The guest bathroom didn't tempt him. Nor did Lily's room, though the door was open and he was briefly nonplussed by a pair of eyes glittering in its curtained darkness: a rocking horse. The room Charlie used for an office had even less allure; almost a kind of anti-magnetism, as though walled in the aura of faint tedium that Charlie's existence, rich and privileged as it was, often seemed to give off. The master bedroom was next. He paused before opening the door, frowning. Further justification seemed required by some scrupulous inner agency before he could allow himself to proceed. *Evidence*, he found himself thinking. Some vital evidence that might, in spite of all indications to the contrary, exonerate Chloe, could be lying around somewhere. What if he were wrong about everything after all, and was at the point of jeopardising, possibly even sacrificing, his two most precious relationships because of some absurd misreading of the situation? Didn't he owe it to himself – to everyone in fact – to go forward?

Dubious as he felt it to be, the formula enabled him to lift the old-fashioned black iron latch. Pushing the door open, he seemed to step into a tumult of scents, colours, emotions, too overwhelming to allow any action to occur other than a kind of stupefied swaying, and any observation other than that of his own reeling dizziness. The question of a search, methodical or otherwise, was gone from his mind, utterly eradicated, as if it had never been present. He took in the fact that the bed was unmade, the floor either side of it strewn with books, magazines, dishevelled bathrobes and pyjamas. Laundry spilled from a basket in the adjoining walk-in closet, under racks of jackets and skirts. His eye skimmed it and in his hand a moment later was a pair of silken underwear, insubstantial as a mist-net but charged with forces that had set his heart slamming in his chest. Jesus Christ, he thought. This was not what he wanted to want. He remembered an exchange with his father: one of their very last, as it happened. Charlie, recently arrived in their household, had been overheard somewhere using the phrase 'jerking off', not at that time a common expression in the British lexicon. Later, in private, Matthew's father had asked Matthew what it meant. Embarrassed, Matthew had explained, and his father, taken aback, had reacted with the words: 'That's something I hope you'll never do,' an injunction that might have been forgotten had he not disappeared so soon after, but that, by virtue of its timing, had taken on the gravity of a biblical commandment, forever conjoining the activity it proscribed with a feeling of burning shame. Even allowing for the more relaxed and modern attitude Matthew had absorbed over time from more enlightened sources (and which he guessed his father himself, had he been caught less off his guard, might well have professed), the exchange had infected Matthew with an irrational disgust for the act, which, one way or another, all too often took the form of self-disgust. He tossed the garment back into the froth of Turnbull & Asser shirts and Lanvin yoga pants and walked quickly out of the room, thoroughly unnerved at the devious machinations of his own mind in bringing him up there in the first place.

Downstairs he went immediately outside to the truck and drove into town, heading straight for Veery Road. This, he realised, was what he had really been wanting to do all along.

The LeBaron was in the driveway of the A-frame. The Lexus was behind the office buildings at the end of the road. So much for the photographic expedition to Fletcher Road. It was exactly as he had foreseen. And yet, again, it gave him a jolting shock to see the imagined act made literal.

Evidently Chloe had gambled on no one taking her up on her invitation to join her out at the mailbox. Or else she'd just counted on being able to brazen it out, somehow, if they did and found she wasn't there.

He drove back to the house – what else was there to do? – and started on the dinner. Having failed to find cartridges for his foamer that morning, he'd put white beans in a crockpot of stock with two heads of garlic and a half-pint of olive oil and managed to find a leg of lamb that didn't look as if it had spent the last decade on the high seas in a refrigerated shipping container. What he had in mind was a simple *gigot d'agneau aux haricots*, the leg hot-roasted country style to make the fats run gold under the crisped parchment of skin while the meat stayed tender and pink. He'd first tasted the dish at the Trumilou in Paris when he and his father had taken their trip around Europe. The combination of the tongue-thick slices of succulent meat, with the soft beans in their creamy juices, had made a powerful impression on him; both elements so robust his mouth had felt as if it were at the confluence of two big rivers of flavour, and it was one of the first dishes he had set out to master when he became a chef.

He studded the joint with rosemary sprigs and rubbed it with lemon juice (in Iceland they glazed it with coffee, something he'd always meant to try), and started to prepare a fricassee of oyster mushrooms for the appetiser. The previous day he'd given a ride to a hitch-hiker, a barefoot young guy who reeked of pot and was trying to sell wild mushrooms to the local stores. Matthew had asked what he had, and he'd opened the sack he was carrying, filling the truck cabin with the loamy pungency of what he assured Matthew were chanterelles, something he called 'Chicken of the Woods', and oyster mushrooms. The latter had looked safely unambiguous and Matthew had bought the lot.

He got a vegetable bouillon going and went down to the cellar: the recipe called for some Muscadet. Being in the basement, which was very much Charlie's domain, got him thinking of their discussion earlier, or rather of his failure, once again, to open the real subject he'd wanted to discuss. He wondered if he'd just been plain wrong about Charlie seeming uneasy when Chloe left. Either way, it was pretty obvious he wasn't ready to hear that his wife was cheating on him, and as Matthew found what he was looking for – a 2008 Domaine de l'Ecu – and carried it back upstairs, he found himself reversing his earlier resolution to take a more direct approach, deciding once and for all (or so he hoped: he knew from past experience that these mental circlings of his had a way of defying all efforts to stop them once they started) to ignore things and just enjoy the summer.

None of my business, he told himself as he diced the shallots and began wiping clean the shelving clumps of oyster mushrooms. *None of my business*, as he debated whether to run out in the truck again on what would almost certainly be a fool's errand to track down some real cane sugar in the 'ethnic' aisle at the grocery store or stay put and hope the so-called brown sugar in Charlie's pantry, which would almost certainly be white sugar sprayed with molasses, would make a not too calamitous substitute for *cassonade*.

He was aware that he could get a little obsessive at times about the finer points of his recipes. It was his own kind of Zen practice, in a sense. What all the niceties of bamboo breathing, positive versus absolute *Samadhi* and so on were for Charlie, balanced flavours and correct technique were for him. The patient pursuit of culinary perfection was his way of escaping his own 'wandering thoughts' and achieving the no-mind state of *Mushin*. At any rate the little mantra, *none of my business*, seemed to be working, and as he assembled the fricassee he felt a welcome blankness descend.

But it didn't last long. Without warning his calm was shattered by one of those waves of apprehension that render entirely futile any notion one might have of being able to master one's own mind. With it came an image of Chloe and her lover fucking in the A-frame, and the realisation that however much he might wish to ignore what she was doing, it was going to be impossible.

Yes, it was none of his business; it was Charlie and Chloe's business alone. And yet it was his own sense of reality that was being threatened. The geometry of his relationship with Charlie and Chloe might shift as one of them drew closer or further away, but it was permanently and exclusively triangular. Inconceivable, somehow, had been the possibility of a fourth figure breaking open this shape altogether, and the intrusion of such a figure was proving remarkably difficult to accept. It was like having to believe, suddenly, in a fourth prime colour, or a second moon.

Charlie returned from his wine tasting a little before eight. He came into the kitchen carrying a mixed case of burgundies and looking much happier than he had before.

'Let's open one of these babies, shall we? What's for dinner?'

'*Gigot d'agneau.*'

'Aha!'

Charlie selected a bottle from the box and uncorked it.

'I love your *gigot d'agneau.*'

'Thanks.'

'Here.' Charlie poured him a glass. 'Cheers.'

'First time I had it,' Matthew said, 'was with my dad, on our trip across Europe. It made an indelible impression on me.'

'Oh?' Charlie composed his features into a look of polite interest. It always seemed to make him nervous to hear Matthew talking about his father. Usually Matthew avoided the subject, but occasionally he felt a perverse desire to bring it up, unfurl it like an old rug and waft its mildewy odours in Charlie's direction. He wasn't sure why. Certainly he didn't regard Charlie as implicated in any way in his father's misfortunes. Not even Charlie's father, Uncle Graham, could really be held responsible for them. True, in his informal capacity as the family's financial advisor he had talked Matthew's father into taking advantage of the new terms by which Lloyd's was making it possible for middle-class investors to join its hitherto exclusively super-rich club of 'names'. But there was never any suggestion that he had any inkling of the Armageddon of claims about to descend on the company, or that he stood to profit by recruiting his brother-in-law. And even if privately, irrationally, Matthew's father did accuse his brother-in-law of all kinds of heinous treacheries and deceptions, obviously Charlie himself, a boy at the time like Matthew, had nothing to do with it.

Still, as Matthew knew from his own experience, a father's deeds have a way of lingering in the psychic atmosphere of their offspring. Which was perhaps why Charlie was looking so uncomfortable right now. The contented air he'd come home with had left him. He gave the impression that he would have liked to remove himself from Matthew's presence, and yet he seemed at the same time transfixed, his wine glass stalling in the air as he waited, head bowed, to hear what else Matthew might be about to bring up from the past.

But in fact Matthew had had no clear motive in bringing up his father in the first place, and seeing Charlie's discomfort, was as eager to move away from the subject as Charlie was.

'Anyway, it should be ready in about twenty minutes,' he said.

Charlie's tension seemed to lessen.

'Sounds good.'

'I assume Chloe'll be back by then . . .?'

'I would think. Magic hour's pretty much over.' Charlie checked his watch and looked out at the sky, from which the pink evening light had almost drained.

'I think I'll sit outside for a bit,' he said.

He crossed the terrace and turned towards his meditation garden. Passing between tall viburnum bushes, he checked his watch again, and disappeared from view.

He was very attached to that watch, a Patek Philippe Calatrava that had belonged to his father. It had a loud tick and Matthew had often wondered how Charlie could get into any serious *Samadhi* state with that racket going on.

Chloe came home as Matthew was putting the finishing touches to the dinner. She seemed at once fragile and elated: full of smiles and clearly wanting to share her joy, though just as clearly at a loss how to do so without giving herself away. Her solution seemed to be an exaggerated all-round friendliness. She watched Matthew with a fond smile as he finished the fricassee.

'We're so lucky', she said, 'to know someone who cooks as well as you do, Matt.'

His heart swelled, helplessly. Fu waddled in, and instead of ignoring him as she usually did, Chloe knelt down and hugged him. Rolling onto his side he made a quiet crooning that sounded like the expression of feelings remarkably similar to Matthew's own at that moment: a grief-suffused love.

'Did you get what you were looking for?' he asked.

Her look of joy faded, and he immediately regretted forcing her back into her lie.

'I think so,' she said.

He thought of asking her if he could see some of the pictures, but he didn't quite have the nerve. Besides, he assumed she'd fob him off with some story about not having taken any digital photos, even though he knew for a fact that she always shot on both digital and film.

But a few minutes later, when Charlie came in, she took one of her digital cameras out of its case.

'Here, Charlie.' She turned on the monitor. 'This is where I was.' She glanced at Matthew, and it seemed to him she must have sensed his suspicions.

Charlie scrolled through the pictures.

'Very pretty,' he commented.

'Take a look, Matt,' Chloe said. 'This was your idea, don't forget.'

She held the monitor up to Matthew. His heart gave a brief lurch, as if there might be a reason to expect anything other than what she showed him. It was just a mailbox on a country road by a cornfield, with a red-and-white Dutch barn in the background. The mailbox itself was an old-fashioned grooved metal canister painted in bright enamels with a picture of baby turkeys following their mother past a simple rendering of the same cornfield and barn. On the rustic wooden stand to which it was fastened, a clay flowerpot with a midnight-blue petunia plant had been set. Low sunlight, coming in gold across the cornfield, made the tangled flowers glow above the little scene, and the whole image was given an extra, jewel-like gleam by the monitor's liquid-crystal display.

'There,' she said, smiling gently at Matthew, and he felt like a jealous husband who has just been offered an acceptable alibi and finds himself pathetically grateful for it, even though he knows perfectly well he is still being lied to.

It really was as if he had become Charlie's stand-in; a kind of surrogate cuckold, condemned to feel all the injury but deprived of any means of doing anything about it, even protesting.

The pictures had all been taken in the same light. Chloe must have dashed out after her assignation at the A-frame to snap them before coming home.

Seven

At the beginning of August Chloe's cousin Jana and her husband Bill rented a house on Lake Classon, a half-hour's drive from Aurelia. They arranged to visit one afternoon, along with another couple who were staying with them.

It was a hot, clear day. They brought their swim things and everyone splashed around in the pool for a while, drinking cocktails.

Jana taught psychology at a college in New Jersey. She had a round face, nothing like Chloe's, and plump thighs that she wrapped in a towel as soon as she got out of the water. She seemed in awe of her beautiful cousin, nodding enthusiastically at everything she said. Chloe, smiling her hostess smile, asked after family members.

Bill, grey-haired, with a small snub of a nose that looked like a baby's, was a political consultant. He and Charlie floated off on inflatable armchairs into a corner where Matthew heard them comparing different news networks' coverage of the Libor scandal.

The couple they'd brought along turned out to be English. Hugh was a writer of some kind, teaching for a term at Jana's college. He seemed good-natured if somewhat abstracted; his eyes partially obscured by thick round glasses. Not shy exactly, but quiet, and rather serious, and apparently oblivious to the heat, judging from the thick tweed jacket he'd arrived in. George, as the woman called herself, owned a vintage clothing shop in London. She was tall and bony, with blades of straight black hair, and spoke in what seemed a cultivated cockney accent, her thin mouth accentuated by bright lipstick. For a while the two of them and Matthew gravitated together, swapping stories of the expat life.

'I was going out of my effing box by about March this year,' George said. 'I thought winter was finally ending. And then the blizzards began! It was fun for about fourteen seconds, then you realise all it is is just piles of useless white gunk that just sit there getting covered in dog shit and soggy fags.'

'That's why people go to Florida,' Hugh said. 'Snowbirds, I believe they call them.'

'Yuk. Florida? Yuk.'

'Or the Caribbean,' Matthew said, pronouncing it in the American way.

'Car*ib*bean?' George mimicked. 'Don't give me that! You're as bloody English as I am!'

'All right, Carib*be*an.'

'Do you know it?' Hugh asked.

'A little.'

96

'I'm curious to go there but I'm told it's mostly been ruined.'

'We used to go to one of the smaller islands when I was a boy,' Matthew said. 'Apparently it hasn't been developed much even now. There's still no airport.'

'Oh, yes? Which one is that?'

Matthew hesitated.

George immediately splashed water at him.

'You don't want to tell us, do you! He doesn't want to tell us. Thinks we'll cause an airport to be built and fill the place with Eurotrash.'

Matthew, who had been thinking exactly that, grinned and told them the name.

'Never heard of it,' George said. 'Must be crap!'

She swam off, laughing.

'I should start the grill,' Matthew said, not wanting Hugh to feel obliged to linger. To his surprise Hugh said he'd help.

'I think I'll get dressed though, first.'

Matthew waited while Hugh changed in the pool house, emerging in his jacket and trousers and a pair of heavy brown brogues.

A silence fell on them as they went out through the pool gate and crossed the lawn towards the grill. Matthew, feeling he was in some sense the host, decided it was up to him to break it. He asked Hugh what books he'd written.

'You're not supposed to ask writers that,' Hugh said, smiling.

'Oh. Why not?'

'Because nine times out of ten you won't have heard of any of them, which leaves you feeling like an idiot and the writer feeling like a failure.'

Matthew laughed. 'Sorry!'

'But the answer is books on social history. I wrote one on the British slave trade. One on the Sheffield Radicals.'

'I'm not sure I . . .'

'Oh, no one's heard of them. They were part of the working-class anti-slavery movement at the end of the eighteenth century.'

'Interesting.'

'Another one on Chartist strikes and insurrections . . .'

They reached the grill area, off to the side of the terrace. Matthew opened a sack of charcoal and tipped the lumps into an aluminium chimney. Hugh sat down on the pile of flat stones Charlie was planning to use for his pizza oven (they'd lain there untouched since Matthew had carried them over from the truck two weeks ago).

'So . . . revolution,' Matthew said cautiously; 'that's your basic subject?'

'Well, exploitation primarily. I think it's a more complex phenomenon than people realise. But yes, revolt also. What about you? What's your . . .'

'Restaurant business,' Matthew said, but not wanting to get into a conversation about his ailing career, added quickly, 'Am I allowed to ask if you're working on something now?'

Hugh shrugged, his large shoulders conveying a sort of burdened but stolid patience. He was surprisingly –

considering his sensitive-looking eyes – thickset and stocky. His steel-tinged brown hair hung in a pudding bowl and looked as if it had been hacked into that shape by a pair of blunt gardening shears. His skin was mealy and pale.

'Oh, I always have a few little projects on the go. There's a more cultural-historical sort of book I'm thinking of calling *The Last Taboo*, about money – how it affects the consciousness of people who have it, or work with it.'

'Like my cousin Charlie?' Matthew said, lighting the paper under the charcoals.

Hugh nodded. 'I was certainly curious to meet him.'

'Not that he's your average money person though,' Matthew put in, a little defensively. He'd formed the idea that Hugh must be some kind of rearguard Marxist. He had a vague sense of the glamour socialism still possessed among the more cultured of his former compatriots; that it was far from being a dirty word, as it was in America.

'In fact he sees himself pretty much in opposition to the archetype.'

Hugh smiled – amiably enough:

'That's good.'

'Where does the taboo part come in?'

Hugh thought for a moment.

'Put it this way, it's the only subject left that celebrities don't talk about in their memoirs. Their *own* money, I mean. They'll come clean about all the things that used to be taboo – sexual proclivities, drug habits, petty crime – brag about them, in fact. But they don't talk about their money and we don't expect it of them. It's the one subject that's still off-limits. Probably because unlike sex and drugs it's inextricably connected to the one source of guilt and shame that actually has some objective validity, namely the sense that you've stolen another person's labour – cheated them out of their own bodily and mental exertions. All those other forms of shame are basically just masks for this one, in my view; ways of not thinking about the one thing we all know in our hearts to be unequivocally wrong.'

Matthew nodded, fanning the chimney with an old copy of the *Aurelia Gazette*. He wasn't sure he understood what Hugh was getting at, but he was enjoying the sensation, rare these days, of being taken for an educated man of the world. It wasn't how he thought of himself, exactly. His shambles of an education had seen to that, and he tended to be on his guard whenever the talk took an intellectual turn. But this thoughtful compatriot, with his worn old jacket and out-of-season shoes, put him at his ease.

They chatted on until the others came over from the pool, and for the next hour Matthew was in and out of the kitchen, busy with the dinner. Charlie and Chloe had made it clear they wanted a casual, no-frills barbecue, which was fine with him, but he was damned if he was going to serve up store-bought hamburger buns or ketchup, so there was all that to see to as well as getting the grill-rack brushed and oiled and heated to the right temperature. As he was taking the brioche dough out of the fridge, George appeared in the kitchen.

'So what exactly is your gig here, then?' She perched tipsily on a stool. 'Are you the English butler or something?'

Matthew explained that he was here as Charlie's cousin and old friend but also happened to be the designated chef.

She chuckled.

'So democratic, the American class system. Right?'

He made a non-committal sound and began shaping the brioche buns.

'No, but seriously, what is your racket?'

'You mean in general?'

'Yeah, whatever . . .'

'Not much right now,' Matthew said. Then, not wanting to come off as a complete nonentity, he told her about his plan for a gourmet food truck.

'How Brooklyn! What would you make?'

'I'm thinking maybe *pupusas*.'

'What the *fuck* is a *pupusa*?'

Matthew explained, adding, 'It probably wouldn't work in England.'

'You'd have to call it a *pupusa* buttie . . .'

He smiled. 'Anyway, it's strictly a pipe dream till I figure out how to get my hands on a truck.'

'And how much would that set you back?'

'Forty, fifty grand, for anything halfway decent.'

'Fuck!'

'Right.'

'Better hit up your cousin Charlie! Or have a dig around in one of those sofas – probably a few grand in change right there.' She lowered her voice: 'What's he make all his dosh from, anyway?'

'Banking.'

'Oh, right, Jana said.'

'Plus he inherited a few million.'

She snorted. 'I inherited my mum's microwave.'

'That's more than I got.'

'Really? You sound posh.'

'No more than you, I'll bet.'

'Ooh! I'll have you know that behind this mockney is a genuine cockney. My Auntie Becca was known as the Pearly Queen of Bethnal Green.'

Matthew laughed, warming to her despite her jagged manner. She slid off her stool, waving magenta-nailed fingers at him and swaying a little as she clopped away.

At dinner, after he'd served up the burgers, he found himself seated next to her at the stone table. She was vehemently disagreeing with Bill about an opinion he'd just offered, concerning a well-known TV host.

'Rubbish! He's a prat, Bill. He's a talking colostomy bag, not a journalist. And definitely not "even-handed".'

'Oh, I think he's pretty even-handed,' Bill retorted with a bland smile. He didn't seem terribly enamoured of his house-guest.

'Crap! He's about as even-handed as a fucking . . . lobster.'

'A lobster. That's good, George.'

After they'd finished eating, Matthew slipped away and did some cleaning up in the kitchen. When he went back outside the atmosphere had changed. George was talking loudly while the others sat listening in various attitudes of discomfort. She'd flagged a little during dinner, but now she was blazing away again. Apparently she'd just remembered, again, that Charlie was a banker, and found that she was compelled by her conscience to go on the attack.

'I'm having a go at you, Charlie,' she was saying with a grin, 'but face it, you're no different, *really*, from some mafia boss or Mexican drug lord up here on your mountaintop, are you? Actually, you're worse—'

Bill cleared his throat.

'It's okay, Bill,' she said, 'I'm just having a go at our host. It's very English of me, I know, but Charlie doesn't mind, do you, Charlie?'

'Be my guest.'

'Ha. No, but seriously, you actually *are* worse than a mafia boss or a Mexican drug lord, Charlie, because they at least risk getting killed or locked up for robbing defenceless people of their life savings and stealing their houses, whereas you're not only *allowed* to rob people of their life savings and steal their houses, you are positively *encouraged* to rob people of their life savings and steal their houses. In fact, the more you rob people of their life savings and steal their houses, the bigger your year-end bonus, right? And of course, if it all goes *pear*-shaped, you and your chums in your six-thousand-dollar power suits can just get together with your other chums at the Treasury Department in *their* six-thousand-dollar power suits and arrange for an eighty-billion-dollar bailout, paid for of course by the very people you've

103

spent the last decade robbing and stealing from. Right, Charlie?'

Charlie took a deep breath and exhaled slowly. Chloe was looking at him, as if waiting for him to defend himself. But he said nothing.

Jana, who'd been darting glances at her hosts, said:

'That's kind of a not very nuanced way of looking at the situation, don't you think, George?'

'We've been watching a lot of Occupy footage,' Bill put in, more drily.

'Charlie's totally a supporter of Occupy,' Chloe said. 'Tell them, Charlie . . .'

Charlie frowned. Catching the look, Bill continued:

'Well, no, that wasn't my point. I mean, I give credit to Occupy for bringing their issues into the mainstream, but at this juncture I also think they need to leave off what basically amounts to little more than tomfoolery and let the grown-ups deal with what happens to be—'

'The *grown-ups*?' George interrupted. 'The *grown-ups*?'

'—with what happens to be a highly complex situation—'

'Daylight robbery is *not* complex, and who the fuck are the *grown-ups*?'

'What I'm trying to say is blaming the bankers for the inevitable problems that occur from time to time in a free market is like blaming your stomach when you overeat. It's just facile. It's singling out a small group of mostly honest and decent people, and turning them into scapegoats for the consequences of wanting to have cars

104

and houses and easy credit for everyone instead of just, you know, the lucky few. What I'm saying is we're all implicated.'

'Bollocks. How am I *implicated* when Charlie here sweet-talks some little old lady into signing up for a mortgage she can't afford and then runs off and sells that mortgage on to some thicko pension-fund manager, knowing that the little old lady and all the other little old ladies he's sweet-talked in similar honey-tongued fashion are going to default, and the pension fund is going to go *pear*-shaped, and all the pensioners are going to be living off thin *gruel* for the rest of their days? How am I *implicated* in that, pray tell? What do *you* think, Charlie?'

Again Charlie abstained from comment. His back was straight, his mouth slightly open. Looking at him, Matthew realised it was his meditating posture. Not the full lotus, of course, but the erect spine, the centring of the body mass on the abdominal triangle – the *Tanden* as Matthew had seen it called in the Zen books lying around the house – the belly breathing, regulated so as to achieve *Mushin*, no mind. It was a technique, as far as Matthew understood, for reducing other people to mere disturbances in the visual field.

Charlie did break his silence, however, a little later. George had moved on to the subject of the banks short-selling mortgage-backed securities even as they were aggressively marketing those same securities to their clients, a practice she seemed to consider worthy of a whole new palette of disgust-effects. While she was in full cry, Charlie muttered something which, perhaps because he'd been so quiet until then, caused her to stop mid-sentence.

'Pardon?'

'You're talking about Goldman Sachs,' Charlie said. 'I worked for Morgan Stanley. They didn't do that.'

'Oh!' George said brightly. 'In that case I owe you a massive fucking apology, don't I? Here, darling . . .' Leaning across the table she planted a big kiss on Charlie's lips and sat back, laughing.

The gesture briefly dissolved the tension at the table.

But then Hugh spoke. He'd been drinking steadily all through dinner, and Matthew had assumed he was more or less in a stupor. But that didn't appear to be the case. Quite the reverse if anything.

'Not that Morgan Stanley was a model of rectitude, exactly . . .' he said.

'I wasn't—' Charlie began. Chloe looked at him expectantly but he broke off, seeming to decide in favour of stoical endurance over further argument.

'I've read quite a bit about them,' Hugh said. 'It's a subject that interests me.'

'Uh-oh, Charlie,' George said. 'Now Hughie's having a go at you. This time you're really in trouble!'

Chloe poured herself a glass of wine and looked out across the dark valley, seeming to absent herself. Political debate, with its tedious moral one-upmanship, had never seemed to interest her much, and this too was something Matthew admired in her. It was a kind of cleanness, he'd always thought; a refusal to join in the demeaning parlour game of judging and being judged. No doubt this English couple would dismiss it as the complacency of the over-privileged, but he knew her better than that: she'd have been the same Chloe rich or poor; taking whatever life offered, without guilt, and without envy. He was very certain of that.

'No, but I find it all very intriguing,' Hugh said. 'We tend to see subcultures like Wall Street or Silicon Valley as monolithic entities but in fact they're fascinatingly diverse. Goldman Sachs, as far as I understand it, got its sort of uber-predator edge by recruiting purely on the basis of how clever and hungry applicants were. They filled their ranks with all these high-IQ but completely ruthless young blokes out of projects in the Bronx who'd never had any inhibitions about grabbing whatever they could. Morgan Stanley was more old-school, wasn't it? You had to have connections to get a decent job there, which made the whole operation a bit, well, no offence, Charlie, but a bit less sharp. The only reason they weren't short-selling those securities was that no one there saw the crash coming. Isn't that right? Not that being slower off the mark made them any more ethical – then or now, by all accounts. Didn't they just handle the Facebook IPO?'

'I wasn't there,' Charlie said. 'I left in 2005.'

'Ah. But now when was Eliot Spitzer's thing, the Global Settlement? 2003, wasn't it?'

A guarded look appeared on Charlie's face.

'Around then.'

'Eliot Spitzer!' Bill said, rolling his eyes.

Hugh ignored him:

107

'And didn't Morgan Stanley get the biggest fine of any of them?'

'It's possible,' Charlie muttered.

'I'm fairly certain they did. That's been their racket for quite a while, hasn't it? Getting their analysts to sex up the profile of companies on the verge of going public?'

George broke in:

'Is that what you did, Charlie? Were you an analyst?'

In a breathy voice, Jana said, 'I think we should give Charlie a break, already!'

'Me too,' said Bill.

'I'm curious, though,' George pressed. '*Were* you?'

Matthew happened to turn towards Charlie just then. He was thinking it was high time someone mentioned Charlie's long-established interest in ethical investment, and was intending to mention it himself. But as he caught Charlie's eye, a look of anger, hatred almost, flashed across Charlie's features. It was gone before anyone but Matthew could notice it, but it shocked him. He dropped his glance immediately.

'Yes, I was a telecom analyst,' Charlie said quietly to George.

'*Really?*'

'Come on, guys,' Jana said. 'Let it go.'

There was a silence, long and uncomfortable. In it, the distant sound of drumming wafted in on a breeze.

'What's that?' Jana asked.

Matthew answered:

'The Rainbow people.'

'Who are they?'

'Bums in warpaint,' Bill declared.

'Actually, they're interesting,' Matthew said. Seeing an opportunity to atone for whatever he'd done to upset his cousin, he began talking about his encounters with the Rainbow people at the creek. He'd already told Charlie and Chloe the story of his meeting with Pike and the two girls, but Chloe pressed him to repeat it, laughing again as he described the wizened old guy with his embroidered bag. She, at least, seemed grateful to him for steering the conversation away from banking.

'Tell them about those words they use,' she said, smiling at him. 'They have their own vocabulary for everything.'

He rattled off as many of the words as he could remember. Hugh took out a notebook and asked him to repeat them.

'That's priceless,' he said, writing them down. 'Absolutely priceless.'

'Now Hughie's going to write an article about them,' George said, 'and everyone's going to think we spent our time in America living in a fucking teepee!'

A more relaxed conversation developed. Charlie brought out liqueurs and Bill produced some medical-grade pot. The moon rose from behind the mountain, newish, and bright enough that even its dark part had discernible substance and shape. By the time the party broke up everyone was behaving as if nothing untoward had happened.

*   *   *

Later that night, Matthew heard a sound from the pool. He got up and looked out of the guest-house window. Charlie was in the water, swimming the steady, head-down crawl he used for doing laps. Reaching the end he turned, plunging back the other way; his long, straight body cutting the same undeviating line through the water.

After a while he climbed out and dried off. But instead of going back to the house, he wrapped himself in a towel and sat in a deckchair, motionless. He didn't seem to be meditating. His slumped body suggested something more along the lines of brooding.

The English couple must have left him feeling bruised, Matthew supposed. He thought perhaps he should go down and commiserate. But he wasn't sure how welcome he would be. Charlie had been rather distant with him lately. Borderline unfriendly, in fact. The other day he'd come back from New York in an upbeat mood after a meeting with a former executive from Grameen America, the US branch of the Bangladeshi bank that had pioneered micro-loans, and announced that he was going to adapt their approach for his own investment group (he was no longer referring to this as a 'consultancy' group, a fact Matthew had noted with the faint amusement his cousin so often provoked in him). 'It's exactly what I've been looking for,' he'd told Chloe excitedly. 'It puts money into exactly the kind of small-scale entrepreneurship I've always believed in, and it turns out to be a damn safe bet for investors.' But as soon as Matthew had started asking him questions about it, expecting to join in the conversation, he'd clammed up. And then there'd been that strange look of outright hostility at the table tonight. What had that been about? Matthew wondered. He tried to think what he could have said to provoke it. But he'd hardly spoken at all by that point in the dinner.

On the other hand, it was possible he was just imagining all of it. Maybe the look was just a general expression of irritation that happened to have caught him in its beam. And maybe, by the same token, the other episodes had equally innocent explanations. He did suffer from a certain social hypersensitivity. He'd read somewhere that it was called the 'spotlight effect': a tendency to imagine other people were paying more attention to you than they really were. It made you self-conscious; inclined to attribute critical judgements about yourself to people who in fact weren't thinking about you at all.

Well, if that was all it was, then perhaps he should go down and talk to Charlie after all. Let him know he was on his side, whatever that English couple thought of him.

He put on some clothes and went down the path to the pool. The stars were bright, the midnight air throbbing with drums and katydids.

Charlie looked over as he opened the gate, his face lit by the pool lights.

'What's up?'

'I was wondering if you could use some company.'

'Oh.' Charlie glanced up at the guest-house window.

'I thought you might want to talk.'

'About what?'

The defensive tone stalled Matthew.

'I don't know . . . I thought they might have upset you at dinner – the Brits.'

Charlie shrugged.

'It's not exactly news to me, what they were saying.'

'I guess not.'

Matthew was standing by the pool, uncertain whether to sit down. After a moment Charlie said, very coolly:

'Are you sure that's what you wanted to talk about?'

'What do you mean?'

Charlie stared at him, his smooth features unsmiling. Then he shrugged and stood up, giving a yawn.

'Just wondering.'

'What else did you think I—'

'No, nothing.' Charlie yawned again. 'Sorry. I'm tired.'

'I mean, Charlie,' Matthew persevered, somewhat against his better judgement, 'I'm always happy to talk about anything. You know that. Anything at all . . .'

Charlie smiled.

'I didn't mean that. But thanks anyway.' He turned to go.

'Charlie—' Matthew heard himself blurt. At that moment he was as close as he ever came to telling Charlie about Chloe's lover. He often wondered, later, how things would have turned out if he had.

Instead he broke off. In the silence that followed, Charlie turned to face him again, giving a strange look of sceptical expectation, as if Matthew were in the process of fulfilling some damning prophecy someone had made about him. It wasn't the actively hostile look of earlier, but there was a total absence of warmth in it. Utterly bewildered, Matthew tried to think of some word or phrase to break the tension, but before he could, Charlie turned the exchange in an altogether unexpected direction.

'By the way, Matt, this is kind of awkward, but we have some friends coming and we're going to need the guest house, just for a few days.'

'Oh . . . No problem. I'll move my stuff into the spare room.'

'No, I mean we need that too. Also Lily's going to be back from camp, so she'll need her room.'

'Oh. Okay.'

'I was thinking maybe if you had things you needed to do in the city, you might want to go down for a few days.'

Matthew didn't know what to say.

'I mean . . . as I think I mentioned, I've sublet my place . . .'

'That's fine. You can stay at the house. No one'll be there. I think it'll just be for three nights, and not for a week or so.'

'Well . . . Okay . . . Thanks,' Matthew said, trying not to feel aggrieved.

'Night then,' Charlie said.

'Goodnight.'

Back in bed Matthew lay awake for some time. Charlie's willingness to send him away in order to make room for other friends, surprised him, but he didn't want to have to feel upset with his cousin. In fact, he wanted very much not to have to feel upset with him, and after a while he was able to persuade himself that from

113

Charlie's point of view, there really wasn't any callousness in it at all. He was just trying to solve a logistical problem.

He closed his eyes and curled up in a determined simulacrum of sleep, furiously barring his consciousness against the mass of thoughts clamouring for entry, until finally real oblivion descended.

Eight

In the morning he found Charlie drinking coffee alone on the terrace. It was early, not yet seven.

'Good sleep?' Charlie asked. Tanned and relaxed in his grey T-shirt and draw-stringed shorts, he seemed fully recovered from his brooding hostility of the night before. His lean legs sprawled forward, feet comfortably crossed at the ankle, tapping each other as if in mutual affection.

'Not bad.'

'Have some coffee.' Charlie nodded at the pot and looked back down at his iPad. He held the device in his left hand and scrolled with his right, dismissing current events that didn't interest him with a flick of his fore-finger, and detaining others with a lightly proprietorial jab as if to say: 'Just one moment, you.'

'Chloe still asleep?' Matthew asked.

'No. She went out. She'll be back with pastries after Early-to-Bread opens.'

'Where'd she go? I mean . . . I mean . . . it's kind of early for yoga, isn't it?'

Charlie looked up.

'She went to take pictures.'

'Ah. More mailboxes.'

'Right. She figured she ought to get out there while she still can. Lily'll be home tomorrow.'

'Right. Of course. Make hay while the sun shines. So to speak.'

Charlie gave him another glance, and turned back down to his screen.

'I think I'll get an early start too,' Matthew said.

'Uh-huh.'

'There's a farmers' market in East Deerfield . . . Always good to beat the crowds.'

'Well, don't get anything for me. I'll be in the city.'

'You won't be coming home?'

'Yeah but late, and I won't be eating. There's a dinner.'

'Anything interesting?' Matthew asked, eager to leave but at the same time anxious to ascertain where he stood with Charlie; still clinging to the hope that his cousin's hostility might have been purely imaginary.

'What?' Charlie was looking at his screen.

'Anything interesting – the dinner?'

'Oh, those Grameen people. Ex-Grameen.'

'That sounds encouraging . . .'

'We're getting there.'

'Micro-loans, right?'

'Right.'

'What exactly is a micro-loan? I mean, what sort of sum?'

Charlie looked up at him.

'It varies.' He seemed on the point of getting annoyed. Bewildered, Matthew dropped it.

'Well . . . See you later, then.'

'See you later.'

He drove fast, making the turns without thinking. The LeBaron was in the A-frame's short driveway, and this time so was the Lexus, squeezed in right next to it, both fenders gleaming in the morning light. The sight was strangely shocking; shattering almost. It was as if, until now, some part of him really had been clinging to a shred of hope that he'd been imagining things. He plunged on past, his head reeling.

So what? he told himself. *Her business not mine.* At the same time, from some ungovernably autonomous region of his mind, other thoughts arose; crushing, and still more crushing. She didn't care anymore if she was found out . . . She *wanted* to be found out; wanted to precipitate a crisis, upend her marriage . . . Or no, she wasn't even thinking about her marriage: she'd just been in too much of a hurry to see her lover, get into his bed for an early-morning fuck on this last day of easy mobility, before her daughter came back from camp. *So what? So what?*

He pulled out onto the County Road and a garbage truck he hadn't seen blasted its horn as it bore down, snorting into his mirror. Shaken, he made an effort to get a grip on himself. After a moment a slightly more rational explanation for the car's presence right there in the driveway came to him: she must have simply thought she was safe from discovery at that early hour. It wasn't much of a comfort, but it countered the suggestion of uncontrollable desire, which made its effect on him less incendiary. The pitch of his own feelings appeared to be connected with Chloe's. If he could tell himself this was just an ordinary affair pursued out of ordinary boredom, and regulated by sensible caution, he felt he could manage this absurdly inappropriate anguish.

He was driving towards East Deerfield because he had told Charlie he was going to the farmers' market. But he didn't feel like going to the farmers' market and it wasn't as if Charlie would give a damn whether he went to the farmers' market or not. What he felt like doing, he realised, was going back to Aurelia, back to the A-frame. The further away he got, the more strongly he felt drawn back to it, as if distance brought out some mysterious soothing essence lodged in that triangular building that wasn't discernible in the tumult of things he felt in its proximity. At the same time the very urgency of the desire to go back seemed reason enough to resist it. It was abundantly clear to him that he was becoming unhealthily fixated on that little house.

He turned off the County Road and drove aimlessly along the winding lanes that spread through an area of old dairy farms. Some of these looked abandoned; broken barns standing open to the sky, machines rusting in tall weeds.

I should leave right away, he thought; not wait till Charlie's guests arrive. Just make my excuses and go.

But where? His own apartment was sublet. His few friends aside from Chloe and Charlie were all dispersed for the summer. In the past he would have gravitated towards the house in Spain, near Cádiz, where his mother and her third husband spent their summers, but his mother had died two years ago, and the husband, who owned the house, hadn't seemed interested in continuing his relationship with Matthew. He could visit his sister, he supposed. She and her partner, both social workers, lived in Bristol, a city he liked. But they were religious and the last time he'd visited, almost ten years ago, their determination to drag him off to church had got on his nerves. He could go somewhere on his own, of course, but that would mean motels and restaurants, which would eat up the meagre profit he was making on his sublet; money he was counting on to help get him through the rest of the year.

The rest of the year . . . It was only the second week of August but suddenly he was aware of autumn. The leaves overhanging the narrow roads were dusty and frayed. The grasses already looked dry. And still he had made no progress in the task he'd set himself, of getting to grips with the curious stalling paralysis that had taken him over.

Part of the problem was that he'd counted on being able to talk to Charlie and Chloe about it, but in their different ways they'd both made themselves inaccessible. Not that he blamed them, he assured himself, fighting off an urge to do just that. Why should they concern themselves with his private problems?

I should leave, he told himself again; find a cheap motel on the Jersey shore and hole up for the rest of the summer.

He'd come to an area of cultivated fields, with split-rail fences dividing them. A red Dutch barn came into view as he drew level with a well-tended cornfield. It looked oddly familiar, and he realised it was the one Chloe had photographed the other day. He slowed down. There was the mailbox with the enamel-painted wild turkeys and the petunia in its clay pot. The thought that Chloe had been here with her cameras, gave the little scene a poignancy that clutched at him. He stopped and got out of the truck, breathing in the warm, sweetish air. The sense of her was strong suddenly, saturating, as if he had come upon yet one more of those secret pockets of hers. He felt close to her, standing where she had stood; linked across the intervening days as if by hidden threads, like the threads at the back of a tapestry. The corn stalks were taller than he was, armed in their heavy cobs with the yellow silks blackening where they spilled from the split sheaves. At the edge of the field, blue starry flowers – cornflowers, he supposed – stood out against the steel-green darkness of the corn. Their blue looked warm at first, but the longer he looked the colder it seemed to grow, as if it too were an incursion from the future; a backward glance of arctic blueness from the winter ahead. He climbed into the truck and headed back towards Aurelia. It was past eight by the time he got there: Early-to-Bread would have opened. It occurred to him that, assuming Chloe had left, he could go and knock at the door of the A-frame; pretend he'd been sent by the owner of the house to check the furnace or look at a crack in the ceiling. The guy would have no reason not to let him inside.

But then what? he wondered, frowning in bewilderment at the scenario he'd created. Why would I want to get inside?

The Lexus was gone from the driveway when he reached the A-frame. He slowed, looking in through the blur of a screened window. A light was on. A large head moved against it.

Matthew sped away, his heart racing.

Charlie had left for New York when he got back to the house, and Chloe was out by the pool. The breakfast things were still on the stone table, and Matthew cleared them away. A half scooped-out cheese sat on the kitchen counter, oozing from its cavity. Matthew threw it out and put the dirty plate and spoon in the dishwasher. He couldn't help disapproving of the wastefulness of his cousin's habits. He would pick up novelty loaves from Early-to-Bread on his way home from tennis, bite off a chunk, and let the rest go stale in the back of his car. Or he'd buy plastic-encased raspberries and leave them around unopened till they grew a fur of mould.

The landline rang. Matthew picked up: it was Jana, wanting to speak to Chloe. He called out to the pool and Chloe came in, putting on a pale blue shirt over her swimsuit. Matthew stood out on the terrace while she talked.

After she'd finished she came outside.

'Matt, I'm going out for the evening. Jana invited me over for a girls' night. Bill's away.'

'Ah. Okay.'

She stepped close to him under the grape arbour. 'Sorry to be deserting you.'

'Don't be silly.'

'I hope you weren't planning something special, for our dinner?'

'No, no.'

The truth was he'd barely taken in the fact that they'd been supposed to have dinner alone that night, so estranged had he been feeling from her.

'I'd much rather stay here with you,' she said, 'but I think Jana's having marital troubles.'

'No problem.'

She put her hand on his arm.

'You should go out somewhere too, Matthew. Have a change of scene.'

He looked at her, surprised at the sudden solicitousness.

'The bar at the Millstream's supposed to be fun,' she said, grinning. 'You should check it out. You might meet someone.'

'Hey! Who says I want to?'

Chloe laughed, her small teeth flashing white. She opened the kitchen door. 'Shall we have some iced tea?'

'Sure.'

'Seriously, Matt. It would do you good,' she said, coming back with the glasses of tea on a tray.

'To pick someone up at a bar? That's never really been my thing.'

She looked at him across the stone table; the uncluttered beauty of her face with its expression of tender attentiveness pure pleasure to behold.

'I don't know – I remember a time when you had a new girlfriend every time we met . . .'

'Well, I didn't pick them up at bars!'

'What about that blonde you met at Rucola?'

'Alison? She was eating there, at the table next to me. Not the same as a bar pickup.'

Chloe's cell phone made a sound. She ignored it.

'Okay, but wait, there was one actual bartender, wasn't there?'

'Yes. I met her at the Nitehawk Cinema.'

'Right. I liked her. But I preferred the blonde. I'll tell you a secret – Charlie and I were actually hoping you might settle down with her. She seemed just right for you.'

'How so?' Matthew asked, pleased by this evidence of interest in his emotional well-being, even though it was from several years in the past.

'Well, she was cheerful and, I don't know . . . easy-going. Wasn't she from the West Coast? Charlie said he could see the two of you running some nice little café together, in Portland or somewhere. Her at the front, and . . .'

'Me skulking at the back?'

'No! You doing the cooking. I thought she was perfect for you.'

'I'm not sure I'd have been perfect for her, though . . .'

'Oh, who cares? You should only ever consider your-self when it comes to love. You think I ever cared if I was right for Charlie? No! I saw he was right for me and I pointed myself straight at him! And I've never regretted it.'

Matthew laughed, ignoring the urge to ask why she was cheating on him in that case, so happy was he to be talking the way they always used to; light and bantering, and coolly frank. Already he could feel her familiar, clarifying effect on him. She had a way of restoring him to himself; an intuitive understanding of his deepest nature that he'd never encountered in anyone else.

'Anyway,' she said, 'I don't necessarily mean getting a date. I just mean you should go out, talk to people, see some new faces, cheer yourself up. That's all.'

'Why? Do I seem unhappy?'

'No. Just a bit . . . locked up in yourself.'

'Hmm.'

'Hmm what?'

'Well, I have been feeling a little bit . . . locked up. It's been bothering me, actually.'

'Really? You should have told me.'

'Oh . . . I don't want to burden you with my woes.'

'Come on! What are friends for? Tell me about it.'

'Well . . . It's nothing very specific, just a sort of . . . stalled feeling . . . If that makes sense . . .'

'When did it start?'

'I think around the time I sold my share in that restau-rant. You remember . . .'

'I do. You were going to invest in some other project. What happened to that?'

'I'm not sure . . . I think I just . . .' He groped for words to express the strange loss of will that had begun afflicting him. It was an elusive subject, however, a process spread over time that had never quite crossed the boundary from the possibly imaginary to the definitely real, and anyway seemed not to want words to express it so much as a kind of childish sob of anguish which he now found himself, to his embarrassment, suddenly struggling to contain.

Chloe's cell phone made another sound and this time she glanced at it. Picking it up from the table, she walked away, signalling she'd just be a minute. She stopped a few yards off and listened, saying nothing. Then she walked briskly further off, passing through the apple trees to the pool, and shutting the gate behind her.

Matthew took the opportunity to pull himself together. Much as he'd been longing for the opportunity to talk like this, he didn't want to make a fool of himself. The last thing he needed was for Chloe and Charlie to start thinking of him as an actual basket case, which would be the inevitable consequence if he gave in to this sudden mortifying impulse to weep. A drily ironic attitude to one's own pain was, he knew, the only safe way of discussing it.

The emotions that had ambushed him had their origins in events from long ago; he was well aware of that. They had lived inside him for almost three decades, with an undiminished power. For periods they were dormant, but when they surged up like this, they could be overwhelming, and it was only with a determined effort that he was able to subdue them, fighting them back until he had achieved the requisite counterbalancing state: an arid indifference to everything.

Several minutes had passed, and Chloe was still on the phone. He could see her in glimpses between the apple trees, pacing around the pool, and he could hear her voice, rising intermittently between long silences.

It came to him that his reaction to her infidelity had something to do with these unmastered childhood feelings. Pursuing the intuition in Dr McCubbin's prescribed manner, he found himself forming the surprising thought that he was indeed experiencing jealousy: not from the point of view of his actual self, but the self he would become if he were ever to be freed from the grip of those ancient emotions. Because that other, freer self regarded Chloe as nothing less (a look of amusement spread on his face as he articulated this thought) than his own true wife. Charlie, at that imaginary juncture, would be nothing more than a minor inconvenience. All this belonged, of course, to a purely latent version of reality.

When Chloe finally reappeared, she had put on sunglasses. She smiled as she approached the terrace, but she'd tightened into herself, gripping an elbow with one hand.

'I'm sorry that took so long.'

'Everything okay?'

'Yes.' She looked away, and then turned back to him.

'Actually, Matt, I have to go out for a bit. Do you mind?'

'Of course not.'

She moved off quickly, as if afraid he might question her, grabbing her car keys from the kitchen table.

'We'll finish our talk another time, right?' She was still in just her shirt and swimsuit.

'Absolutely.'

A moment later, he heard the Lexus start up and accelerate off down the driveway.

The silence of their aborted conversation reverberated in her wake. It seemed to press against him, pushing him into the house, and then out again. He went to the pool and lay on the wooden sunbed Chloe had vacated earlier. Its warm laths smelled of her sun-oil. Butterflies hovered on the zinnias and cleomies. It came to him once again that he should pack his things and leave. Chloe could drop him at the green on her way to Jana's this evening, and he'd wait for the bus . . . He got up from the sunbed and climbed the rocky path to the guest house, trying to think of a plausible excuse for his departure.

But as soon as he entered the pleasant room with its rough plank walls and pine-scented air he changed his mind. What is happening? he thought. What am I doing? He went back to the house. In the cool of the sunken living room he picked up a gigantic volume of Helmut Newton nudes. As he leafed through the long-boned, silvered figures his thoughts moved forward to the moment of Chloe's arrival back from her lover (there was no doubt in his mind that that was where she'd gone), and he felt the impossibility of being able to step back into their briefly revived intimacy. Better not to be here at all when she returned than risk alienating her with the sullenness he was inevitably going to be radiating. He shut the book and went out to the pickup truck in the driveway, dimly aware, as he turned the key in the ignition, of having rationalised a desire he knew to be irrational.

Town was unusually busy, with traffic backed up a quarter-mile from the green. Something was going on in the athletic fields that ran down one side of the road. A stage had been erected, and there was a woman on it speaking into a microphone. As Matthew drew level, her words became briefly audible: '. . . so for those of you who have ever needed the fire company, or enjoyed the flowers on the village green, or had a relative taken care of in the Aurelia hospice . . .' Further along, hanging over the entrance to the field, was a sign reading: '*Volunteers Day Picnic and Fireworks*'.

The traffic eased up after the green, and he was soon crossing the bridge over the creek and turning onto the leaf-dappled twists and turns of Veery Road. The LeBaron was in the driveway. Right next to it, gleaming remorselessly in the hard sunlight, was the Lexus.

He drove on. What now? It was three in the afternoon. He appeared to have exhausted his options. Waiting at the house for Chloe, circling back to the A-frame, packing his things and leaving: every possibility seemed to bring him up against the same intolerable reality.

A band of schoolchildren was on the stage playing 'Crazy Train' as he drove back past the athletic field. Troops of families were gathered before them, cheering them on. Apparently the town had an existence beyond supplying Charlie and Chloe with convenient places to play tennis and conduct assignations.

Back up the mountain, he went straight to the guest house. At least here he felt a degree of calm. He lay on the bed, reaching for his father's old Penguin edition of Pascal's *Pensées*; this also more for purposes of talismanic comfort than any more practical aim.

The book was part of a boxload his mother had sent him when she'd remarried and decided to get rid of his father's things. For a long time Matthew hadn't been able to face unpacking them, but lately he'd begun thinking about his father from the point of view not just of an abandoned child wanting to be magically reunited with him, but of an adult curious to understand him. A year ago he'd started reading through the books, hoping they might have something to offer in this regard. It turned out his father had had a habit of noting the date he'd read each volume, enabling Matthew to follow him in chronological sequence, and giving him the somewhat eerie impression of tracking down his absconded parent along a kind of trail or spoor of print.

As a young man Gerald Dannecker's tastes seemed to have run mostly to English comic novels, full of farcical plot twists and larky repartee. Later, after marrying and settling into his career, he'd begun to read more widely: political biography, travel, popular science. It was in the period following the Lloyd's crash, that the books by Pascal and other philosophers had begun appearing. Having never before been a marker of passages, he had begun carefully underlining pithy phrases during this period, and this gave the books a peculiarly personal aura. Alighting on the markings, which were in pencil and always very neat, Matthew would feel a tantalising proximity to his father's thought processes. The sense of an agitation crystallising, dissolving, reformulating itself, was palpable. From the beginning, the question of suicide had been ominously present. In a book of Schopenhauer's writings Matthew had found underlined: '*Neither in the Old nor in the New Testament is there to be found any prohibition or even definite disapproval of it.*' Several months further along, in a collection of aphorisms by E. M. Cioran, the thought was still clearly on his father's mind, and its coloration had become even more positive: '*Suicide is one of man's distinctive characteristics, one of his discoveries; no animal is capable of it, and the angels have scarcely guessed its existence.*' In the same book, however, the underlinings had directed Matthew to stirrings of what appeared to be an entirely different impulse: '*There has never been a human being who has not – at least unconsciously – desired the death of another human being.*' Disturbed, Matthew had wondered whose death besides his own his father might have been desiring. The directors of Lloyd's? Charlie's father – Uncle Graham – who had talked him into becoming a 'member' of that accursed organisation in the first place? But before he could answer the question, it too had undergone radical twists and refinements, culminating in a passage at once so opaque and so communicative, Matthew had committed it to memory: '*Who has not experienced the desire to commit an incomparable crime which would exclude him from the human race? Who has not coveted ignominy in order to sever for good the links which attach him to others, to suffer a condemnation without appeal and thereby to reach the peace of the abyss?*'

For at least a year after his father had disappeared, Matthew had been certain he was going to contact him, probably with some cryptic message that only Matthew would recognise as coming from him, and that only Matthew would understand. No such message had ever come, and yet as he'd read through this last sequence of books, it had begun to seem to him as if it was after all written right there in those neat pencil lines: just as cryptic as he had always imagined it would be, and at the same time just as powerfully eloquent. By the time of Pascal's *Pensées*, the last in this concluding sequence, the quandary over what course of action to take seemed to have given way to a more generalised mood of reflection and speculation. Perhaps a decision had been taken and his father was merely waiting for the courage, or the right moment, to act.

A coroner's verdict had declared him legally dead after the obligatory seven-year period, but the declaration had been a purely administrative event in Matthew's mind. Unlike his mother and sister who had eagerly accepted the verdict, relieved by this final official purging of the taint of disgrace, Matthew had never been able to assign his father conclusively to the category of either the living or the dead. He thought of him as a kind of vacillating spirit moving between both worlds, and these books had done nothing to settle this uncertainty. It had always been hard for him to accept the banal criminality of his father's deed. Emptying out his clients' accounts! The very fact that he'd had signatory power over these accounts in the first place was proof, surely, of his absolute probity; a measure of how thoroughly out of character the deed had been. And yet the books, with their cunning and convoluted moral arguments, only made it harder to reach any kind of stable verdict. He didn't know what to believe; wasn't even sure what he *wanted* to believe. In one fantasy his father had killed himself but stolen his clients' money first so as to make it look as if he'd just run off somewhere, and thereby spare his family the trauma of his suicide. In another, his father had reached some obscure philosophical justification for the theft and was still alive, living anonymously in some secluded place on the proceeds. Matthew even half-fancied he knew where that place was. There was a turquoise house on the hillside high above the little secluded cove known as Tranqué Bay on the Caribbean island where the family had gone on holiday three winters in a row. Lying in his deckchair, his father used to gaze up and fantasise out loud about living there. 'If we ever come into any serious money,' Matthew remembered him saying, 'that's the house I shall buy.' Matthew had reminded his mother of this at the time of the investigation, and she had passed it on to the detectives from

Scotland Yard. Nothing had come of it, and yet whenever he thought of his father as still living, his imagination persisted in placing him there above Tranqué Bay, enjoying the sea breeze on the carved wooden veranda that was just visible from the white sands below.

Leafing back and forth through the pages as he lay on his bed in the guest house, Matthew read and reread the underlined passages, stalking his father's shade through the thoughts and aphorisms, some of them familiar to him, some forgotten, others encountered now for the first time. He found: '*Incomprehensible that God should exist and incomprehensible that he should not*, and: *All men naturally hate each other.* He found: *Justice is as much a matter of fashion as charm is*, and: *It affects our whole life to know whether the soul is mortal or immortal.*' And with each underlined phrase he felt at once closer to his father, and more baffled by him than ever.

It was six-thirty. He had fallen asleep. The sky over the valley was lilac, with just a few dry-looking clouds. He had dreamed of the cornfield, only he was there with Chloe, and had asked her point blank: Who is your lover? Leaning in so that her hair brushed against his face, she had said softly in his ear: 'I love you,' and he had woken in a burst of happiness.

Through the guest-house window he saw her floating on her back in the pool. He put on some clothes and went down.

'Hi there,' she called. 'I looked for you.'

'I fell asleep.'

'I figured. I was hoping you'd take a walk with me and Fu. Thought we might talk some more. But I didn't want to wake you.'

'I had a dream about you,' he said impulsively.

She hung motionless on the water, her face impassive, and for a moment he wondered if he had transgressed the tacitly agreed-on limit of what could be spoken of out loud between them. But then she smiled.

'Did you? I hope it was nice.'

'It was very nice.'

'That's good.'

He felt suddenly very close to her. God, it was good to have someone in his life he could speak to without inhibition! She didn't ask what had happened in the dream, but her very silence seemed proof that she didn't need to be told, and this surely confirmed that the closeness he felt was real.

That there was something abject, pitiable, in the nourishment he took from such barely discernible signs and tokens of affection, he was well aware. It didn't trouble him, though. He'd learned long ago not to torment himself about things over which he had no control. One went through phases of strength and weakness in one's relation to the world, and when one was in a phase of weakness, as he appeared to be now, there was no sense in pretending otherwise. That was a recipe for humiliation. With luck he would rally himself before long, and then who knew what might happen? In the part of his mind not subject to regular intrusions of rationality there was no doubt at all that his and Chloe's destinies were inextricably linked; even that at some point – in another life if not this one (such concepts were perfectly admissible in this part of his mind) – it had been arranged for them to be together. But in the meantime it seemed important to content himself with whatever crumbs of affection he could glean.

'Want a drink?' he asked.

'No, I should wait till I get to Jana's. Actually, I ought to get going.'

He nodded.

'Everything go okay earlier – in town?' he asked.

'Oh . . . yes.' Chloe plunged forward in the water, submerging her head. Coming up she said, 'Yes, sorry I had to leave so suddenly. It was just this woman I do yoga with. She was in kind of a . . . crisis.'

Matthew looked at her as she shook the water out of her hair.

'Well, I hope you got her sorted, as we say in Blighty.'

'Yes, I did.' A quick smile crossed Chloe's lips. 'I got her sorted.'

'Good.'

'What about you, Matt? Are you going to go out somewhere?'

'I don't know.'

'You should. You should go to the Millstream. It'll do you good.'

'I'll think about it.'

'If you think about it you won't do it.'

She swam over to the chrome steps and climbed out, one hand squeezing the water from her hair.

'Go on,' she said, turning back to him. 'Live a little!'

He'd half-decided to go anyway, and had really only been resisting for the pleasure of Chloe's continued attempt to change his mind.

'All right. I'll go.'

She was upstairs getting ready to go out when he left.

'Let's have a nightcap later on, shall we?' she called down. 'I don't plan on staying late at Jana's.'

'Okay.'

'We can swap notes.'

He laughed.

'Yeah. I'm sure I'll have plenty to report!'

The Millstream Inn was at the low end of town on Tailor Street, just beyond the junction with the County Road. The restaurant was surprisingly crowded considering how early it was, but the bar itself had few customers. It didn't look like much of a pickup scene, Matthew thought, sitting on a stool with a cushioned back. Too early, he supposed. He ordered a gin and tonic and gazed into space, thinking of Chloe's remark that afternoon, about his girlfriends.

It was true that during the years when he'd been part owner of the farm-to-table restaurant, he'd had a period of relative promiscuity. It was something that happened from time to time, without any particular effort or decision on his part; just coming in like the weather. To the extent that he'd analysed it, it was that these were phases when the outward appearance of his day-to-day existence approximated most closely to the generally held idea of what constituted a 'life': regular employment, sustained contact with numerous other people, an overall semblance of purpose. Not that this made him more attractive to women than he normally was: there was the same modest frequency of signals there'd always been, from the same middlingly attractive women who seemed to consider him an appropriate target for their attentions. It was just that during those periods pure sexual need seemed to overcome a certain aesthetic fastidiousness, and he took whatever came his way. Alison, the blonde girl Chloe had liked so much, was plump and highly strung, with a nervous, grating laugh. Chloe's report of Charlie picturing the two of them running some cosy café in Portland had vaguely offended him, though he sensed now that it was the West Coast part of Charlie's fantasy, more than the choice of girl, that had hurt. The suggestion of Charlie wanting to put a few thousand miles between himself and Matthew was upsetting; particularly in the light of Charlie's recent unfriendliness.

He finished his drink and ordered another one. A woman in her forties was looking at him.

'British, right?'

'That's right.'

'I thought I detected an accent. Whereabouts?'

'London.'

'I believe I've heard of it.'

Matthew laughed politely.

'Going to the fireworks?' the woman asked.

It took him a moment to remember the sign he'd seen at the entrance to the town athletic fields.

'Oh . . . I wasn't planning to.'

'Supposed to be a helluva show.'

'Uh-huh?'

'That's what I heard.'

She faced him squarely from her side of the bar, apparently confident in her ability to secure his attention. She wore a pale silk blouse, open to show some cleavage. Her face had a sheen of make-up. Her glistening hair was teased into angled spears like a pineapple top.

She took a sip at her cocktail, setting the near-empty glass down before her with a deliberate air, looking at Matthew. He gave a slight smile and turned away. He was about to knock back the rest of his drink and leave when the door opened and Chloe's lover came in.

Matthew had to remind himself, as the shock jolted through him, that the guy had no reason to know who he was. Trying to appear unflustered, he took a sip from his drink, and laid the glass back down on the bar.

Passing to the other side of the bar, the lover parked himself on a stool, greeting the bartender and extending a general smile all round. He was wearing a loose shirt of white cotton. His beard looked freshly trimmed.

Ordering a drink, he proceeded to offer himself up for conversation with a series of remarks directed at no one in particular. The remarks were cheerfully banal, but soon two guys who'd been talking quietly over beers were laughing with him, and after a while the woman in the pale blouse joined in.

'You going to the fireworks?' she asked.

'Sure am. I have my picnic blanket, my thermos . . . I'm told it's quite the show.'

'Oh, it's fabulous. I go every year.'

The lover looked around.

'Anyone else going? We oughtta form a posse.'

'We're going', one of the two guys said.

'Game on, then! I have time to grab a little something to eat first, right?'

'Definitely.'

The man asked for a menu. Perusing it with a wistful air, he informed the bartender he would just have an appetiser, and ordered a lobster quesadilla.

'But give me a side of the shoestring fries too, would you?'

He added in a stage whisper to the woman: 'My doctor told me I need to gain weight,' prompting a loud, full-throated laugh.

'You here on vacation?' the woman asked.

He nodded.

'Got me a little rental right by the creek there. Veery Road.'

'Nice!'

'The A-frame?' one of the guys asked.

'How'd you guess?'

'The owner's a friend of ours. She has a couple other rentals in town but that's always been the popular one.'

'Easy to see why.'

There was a younger woman, seated to the man's left, whom he hadn't appeared to notice, but now he turned to her, peering closely at the book in her hand. She looked up.

'Oh, I'm sorry, miss. I was just trying to see what you were reading there. I always like to know what books people around me are reading. It's a weakness of mine. Actually, more of a pathological compulsion.'

She held up the book for him to see.

'*Chronicle of a Death Foretold*,' he read. 'Now didn't they make a movie out of that?'

'I don't know.'

'I believe they did. Ornella Muti played the girl, I recollect. I forget the director, but who cares about the director anyhow?'

He chuckled, and the girl smiled vaguely back.

Matthew signalled the bartender for his check. A feeling of restlessness had gripped him: an urge to move. He paid quickly, with cash. Outside, the air was rich with the day's warmth. He saw the LeBaron in the parking lot and glanced in as he walked by; there was a folded tartan picnic blanket on the back seat and a canvas bag with a thermos in it. Climbing into the truck he pulled out onto Tailor Street. The sidewalk was thronged with groups of people, presumably on their way to the fireworks. Traffic heading in that direction was almost at a standstill. He decided to take the back route towards the green, along the other side of the creek. Purely a practical decision, he told himself as he turned onto the County Road and then again onto Veery Road. At the A-frame he slowed down. The driveway was empty and the house was dark – naturally enough, since its occupant was at the bar and Chloe on her way to Jana's. But the urge to stop, to plant himself there, was as strong as it was when he had reason to believe someone was inside. If anything it seemed to be even stronger. He drove on, considering this as one considers a new symptom that has just appeared, of some persistent illness.

Instead of crossing the bridge, he pulled into the stony area just beyond, where people left their cars when they swam. He was in an odd state of mind; at once very conscious of his actions, and extraordinarily detached from them, as though they were being performed by someone else. Parking the truck, he began walking back along Veery Road. Evening sunlight flowed in level rays between the hedges. It was magic hour, he realised, and the thought seemed to plunge him back again into Chloe's aura. He felt as if he were approaching her along some ceremonial, processional route. Pink lilies with long, frilled petals burned like traffic-accident flares above the ditches. The empty-looking houses had molten red suns in their black windows. Ahead of him was the A-frame's sharp tip, pointing up over a tall hedge. He slowed his pace. I am just walking by, he told himself. To do anything different would have required an act of will that he felt safely incapable of mustering. A feeling of extreme passivity had come over him, as though some powerful external process had gathered him into its motions. As he turned left into the short driveway, it was fully in the belief that he was just curious to observe his own feelings at a closer proximity to the place. Even as he lifted the lid from the Weber grill by the screen porch, it was still in a speculative sense; a harmless glancing out across the divide between the actual and

141

the purely conjectural. The door key was under the lid of the grill. As he picked it up, holding it between his finger and thumb, the situation abruptly reversed itself: the same passivity that a moment before had seemed to be keeping him safely from entering the house, was now drawing him inside. No strenuous act of will appeared to be required any longer, or only if he should decide to walk away. It was as if the dense materiality of the little key had sunk the object into him like a fish hook, and he was being reeled in. Already, as he approached the front door, it was the other life, in which he remained outside the house, that was becoming conjectural. This, now, was the actual.

At the same time, he was aware that ever since he had asked the bartender for the check, it had been his intention to do precisely what he was doing.

The door opened into a living area defined by a grey love seat and armchair with a low glass table in between. Beyond the armchair was a fixed wooden ladder leading to a partially enclosed loft under the narrow apex of the roof.

He shut the door behind him, putting the key on a ledge by the doorway, and stepped forward. An air conditioner clicked on.

Passing to the side of the ladder, he saw a door to a room under the loft. He pushed it open. An unmade double bed faced a wall with a narrow window. On the bed was a half-packed suitcase surrounded by piles of folded shirts and pants. Next to it was a desk with a laptop on it. Past the bedroom was a bathroom with shaving things on a shelf over the sink. Beyond, at the rear entrance to the house, was a small kitchen crowded with stainless-steel pans, racks of matching utensils, a wooden knife block and some new-looking appliances.

The glass-paned back door, bolted on the inside, gave onto a stone path across a lawn that dropped off abruptly at what must have been the bank of the creek.

He didn't appear to be afraid. Tense, but not afraid. Even if the man changed his mind about going to the fireworks or decided to come home before, he had his meal to get through first. That ought to keep him at the bar for a good twenty minutes at least, which was plenty of time.

But plenty of time for what? A vague idea of finding out who the man was, had certainly been a part of what had drawn Matthew inside the house, and he looked around for some document, a rental contract perhaps, or some other official piece of paper, that might have the man's name on it. But there was no contract or any other document visible anywhere, and he didn't particularly want to start rummaging in the man's things. Anyway, now that he was here, the question of who the man was didn't seem as pressing as it had. What difference would it make, to know the man's name, or his profession, or anything else about him? Whoever he was, he was the man Chloe loved, apparently more than her husband, and certainly more than Matthew. What could possibly make that fact any more tolerable?

Then why was he here? He wandered back into the living room and sat down in the chair, making a deliberate effort to take stock of things. In the manner Dr McCubbin had taught him, he made himself as fully conscious of the situation he had created, as he could.

What exactly am I experiencing? What do I want?

People who broke into houses usually wanted to take something, didn't they? Or destroy something. Or leave some nasty souvenir of themselves. He didn't seem to have any interest in any of that. What then? Was it just the forbiddenness of being here? The feeling of having attained some secret intimacy with Chloe? Possibly. Certainly he did feel a kind of illicit closeness to her. And yet even as he acknowledged this, he became aware of a lack, an incompleteness in the feeling, and realised that even though he was here, he was still in some mysterious way longing to *be* here; as if inside the A-frame there should have been another A-frame, with another doorway and another key.

He stood up and went back into the bedroom. Something had been nagging at him and he had realised what it was. Half-hidden under the clothes in the suitcase, was a magazine that had caught his eye, though he'd barely been conscious of it. He took it out of the suitcase. It was the entertainment magazine that Chloe had asked him to pick up for her in East Deerfield, earlier in the summer.

He brought it back into the living room, where the light was better, and began leafing through the glossy pages. Near the end, he came to a section headed:

'*Bioflash*'. There, occupying half the page, was Chloe's lover, filling a doorway with his broad frame, gazing cheerfully at the camera.

Holding the page up to the waning light, Matthew began reading the article. It was one of those shamelessly flattering profiles such magazines went in for: calculated to induce envious loathing in even the most well-disposed readers. The man's name was Wade D. Grollier. He was a film-maker. He had been born in rural Georgia in 1978. He lived in Brooklyn with his long-term girlfriend, actress Rachel Turpin (another cheat, then!). He'd had a hit movie that Matthew had heard of, though not seen, about a scientist who creates a robot lover for his daughter. He'd won a Spirit Award, whatever that was, for Best Director. One of his close friends, a Hollywood celebrity, was quoted, describing him as 'an authentic American rebel'. He had spent seven weeks in Haiti after the earthquake, building shelters with his own hands. Before making movies he'd been a rock drummer and he still hung out with rock musicians. Names were given; listed with the deadpan lubriciousness that seemed to be de rigueur in these kinds of pieces.

The ignominy of having been asked to fetch this magazine for Chloe struck Matthew with a belated pang. For a moment he wondered if Chloe had been deliberately amusing herself at his expense; sending the rejected suitor (for they both knew he was that) on an errand to procure this tribute to his triumphant rival. But he quickly dismissed the thought; unwilling to believe she could have been capable of anything so petty, or so deliberately cruel.

The piece continued in the same unctuous style. Wade D. Grollier appeared to be successful modern urbanity incarnate, though at heart he was still a country boy (the piece was slavishly attentive to the formula) and admitted that despite the jet-setting life success had foisted upon him, he loved nothing better than fishing in the head-waters of the Chattahoochee River with his childhood pals. His current project was a cross-species murder mystery set in the jungles of Borneo and featuring an orang-utan detective.

Finishing the article, Matthew went back into the bedroom and returned the magazine to the suitcase. As he'd predicted, knowing who the man was made no difference at all to his feelings about the situation. Nor did the discovery give him any satisfying sense of having accomplished some mission at the house.

He wandered back into the living room. Books, phone chargers, bits and pieces of clothing he hadn't noticed before, lay here and there. None of it looked particularly interesting. On the walls were framed hiking maps of the area, showing streams and trails and tiny black indi-vidual houses among the contour lines of the green-shaded mountains. One of them had the little town of Aurelia itself in an upper corner: a dense sprinkling of black dots spread either side of what must have been Tailor Street, and he was able to trace his way across the creek and down along Veery Road to the bend that came before the A-frame, and then the A-frame itself, where he was standing. It was as though his coming here had fulfilled some already latent itinerary. The downstairs windows were darkening now, but the little loft had a skylight that was still bright. He climbed up the ladder to take a look. Behind the balustrade of carved wooden slats was a plywood floor with a rag rug on it and a rolled-up, single-width futon. The space was probably meant for a child. It clearly wasn't being used.

He sat down on the futon. A flock of birds crossed the skylight, catching the sun on their undersides as they banked upwards. Distant sounds floated over the trees; traffic, a blurred screech of feedback from a PA system. But it was peaceful all the same, up here in the apex of the A, and he felt no urgency to leave. It didn't really seem likely that the man – Grollier, wasn't that his name? – would come home before going to the fireworks, but even the small possibility that he might was of oddly little concern to Matthew. If anything, he noticed, it seemed to excite him fractionally. He found himself toying with the idea of unrolling the futon and staying there all night; not as a serious plan, but with the bemused interest one experiences when an unexpected fantasy lays open some wholly new realm of speculative pleasure.

He was turning over the components of this peculiar fantasy, trying to understand why it should cause this faintly pleasurable apprehensiveness, when he became aware of lights probing down the gravel of the driveway. He knelt up, peering over the balustrade through the front window. He had been in the house barely fifteen minutes! And anyway hadn't he heard the man say he was going straight on to the fireworks? Hadn't he seen for himself the picnic rug and thermos in the car? The lights approached, separating into two beams as they came around the slight curve in the short driveway. Alarm spread through him, and yet for a long moment he did nothing; merely stared into the approaching glare, surrendering to the situation with an almost luxurious helplessness, as if the inertia building inside him all these months had finally rendered him completely incapable of movement. Only by an extreme effort of will was he able to rouse himself. Grabbing the balustrade he hauled himself to his feet and took a few steps down the ladder, trying to calculate whether Grollier would see him if he made a dash for the back door, and whether it would matter even if he did, since he didn't know who Matthew was.

But as the lights went out, he saw that the car itself was not in fact the LeBaron, but the Lexus.

For a moment he thought he must simply be seeing things. In his mind Chloe was so firmly on her way to her cousin Jana in Lake Classon, it was impossible to accept she was here, and he stared, waiting for the hallucination to dissolve. But it was Chloe. He watched her climb out of the car and walk over to the Weber grill, lifting the lid. A puzzled look crossed her face and briefly the hope rose in him that she would leave now. But she put back the lid and, undeterred by the absence of the key, proceeded towards the front door. He stood on the ladder, unsure what to do. If he went any further down, she would see movement through the window. Already she was almost at the door. Only as he heard the handle turn did some dim instinct of self-preservation galvanise him, drawing him back up the ladder and behind the

148

balustrade in time to conceal himself before the door opened.

She had her phone to her ear as she came in. With her free hand she switched on the light. Afraid she might look up and see him between the wooden slats, which were carved at their edges in the shape of ornate brackets, Matthew sat clenched and unblinking.

'Wade,' she said into the phone.

He saw her pick the key from the ledge where he had left it, examine it a moment and set it down again.

'No, I'm at the house . . . Your house, Wade . . . I thought you might want to come say goodbye one more time.'

She was wearing one of her thin, patterned skirts with a short-sleeved top, tailored at the waist.

'I know. I'll call her.'

She moved in quick steps through the room with the phone to her ear, placing her hand lightly on the love seat, the armchair, the side of the ladder. As she moved towards the back of the house, disappearing out of sight, Matthew let himself breathe again. Very carefully, he backed into the corner of the little space, as far as possible from view.

He heard her laugh.

'You know you want to, Wade . . . You know you do . . . Yes, but they never start before ten . . . I know but this is Aurelia. All the bands in town have to do their Jimi Hendrix impressions first . . .'

Then she was directly below him, in the bedroom.

'Oh, Wade,' he heard. 'You really are leaving, aren't you? I'm looking at your suitcase . . . Yes, there's an early bus, around six – easier than driving . . . I know . . . I know, Wade, I do too, but Lily's coming, and anyway, I just can't.'

She came back out of the room, closing the door.

'Be quick, then . . . Okay, but don't feel you have to charm the entire restaurant on your way out. Anyway, did you see Matthew?'

The sound of his own name hit Matthew like an electric shock.

'Yeah, that was him . . . He did? Probably went to the fireworks . . . Well, thanks for going anyway . . . Okay, I'll wait till you get here.'

Something her lover said made her laugh.

'I know. But he can't help that, can he?'

She laughed again, more tenderly. 'Yes, but you're good at sizing people up. Anyway, I thought it might interest you to take a look at him . . . Okay, see you in a bit.'

Back in the living room, she turned off the overhead light and switched on a small table lamp.

Matthew watched her, trying to fathom the implications of what he'd just heard. Now she was on the love seat, facing in his direction, making another phone call.

'Jana? Hi. Listen, I'm so sorry but I'm going to have to be a little late. Some things have come up . . .'

The polite hostess smile Matthew had seen when Jana came to visit, reappeared on Chloe's face. Her small teeth showed like a row of pearls.

'Oh, that's sweet of you . . . No, no, I definitely want to come. I've hardly seen you all summer . . . Thanks, Jana. I shouldn't be too long.'

She stood up and drew the shades down over the living-room windows. Sitting again, she held the phone in front of her face, adjusting her hair and rearranging the rounded collar of her blouse, opening a button to reveal a lacy edge of bra. It took Matthew a moment to realise she was using the phone as a camera to see herself. She put it away in her canvas bag, crossed her legs, and waited. After a few seconds she stood up again and went towards the back of the house, returning with a lit candle in one hand and a small plate in the other, with kumquats on it, and chocolate. She placed them on the glass table, and switched off the lamp. In the candlelight the grey furnishings took on a warmer tone. She stretched, popped a kumquat into her mouth, and lay down on the love seat, closing her eyes. But she was still restless. Standing up again, she slipped her underwear off from under her skirt in a swift, practical motion. Coming around the coffee table, she sat back down – this time on the armchair – and tossed the pale garment onto the floor beside her.

Matthew looked down through the thin gaps, feeling like an animal in a cage. His mouth had gone dry. In the distance he could hear an electric guitar. Closer, katydids had begun their night-time chorus. She had sent her lover to the bar to check him out. Why? he wondered. Am I such a mystery, even to her? Is there something in me I don't see? The question, unanswerable as it was, sent a ripple of anxiety through him.

Headlights pierced through the shades, blading in vertically through the gaps in the balustrade, moving across Matthew's face like a pair of scanners. A moment later the door opened and Grollier stepped inside.

He paused in the entrance, taking in the little tableau Chloe had prepared for him. In silence, he smiled at Chloe across the small room with its flickering gold light. Closing the door behind him, he moved towards her, stooping midway to pick up her discarded panties and fill his lungs with their scent.

Above them Matthew stared down through the slats in the balustrade, scarcely breathing; wanting and not wanting to see.

Nine

An hour later he was still there, his limbs stiffened into position as if he'd been turned to stone, his mind a near blank. Chloe had left, driven off to her cousin, but Grollier was still down there, sprawled naked on the love seat.

Matthew stared down at him. If what he had seen had extinguished any lingering hopes concerning the extent of Chloe's involvement with this man, what he'd heard had spread a deeper, more insidious ruin. It was so disturbing, in fact, that for some time he couldn't bring himself to summon any of it back. He was in a state of benumbed shock. Only some minor functionary of consciousness continued about its business, assessing the practicalities of the situation in a businesslike way: catching the far-off strains of someone's imitation of a Hendrix guitar solo, observing that Grollier would have to leave soon if he was going to make it to the fireworks, noting unexcitedly that this would make his own exit from the house possible.

Grollier stretched and yawned. A smile appeared on his face and he rotated his shaggy head slowly from side to side as if in disbelief at something. Pushing down onto the love seat, he hauled himself up and padded off. Light appeared from the bedroom and Matthew heard drawers being opened and closed. He was getting dressed to go out, surmised the same detached mental functionary. Dully, Matthew projected forward; saw himself finally able to move again, slipping out of the house, driving back up the mountain, continuing with his life. The evening would take its place in the chain of significant episodes that had given his existence its singular character, and there would be no more possibility of forgetting it than there had been any of the others. At the same time it would make no practical difference to anything.

But he was mistaken about Wade getting dressed. The man was still naked when he returned to the living room, and now he began ferrying odds and ends back to the bedroom. It became apparent that he was simply continuing with his packing.

He was flying out to Indonesia tomorrow – Matthew had gleaned this from the post-coital talk – interrupting his stay at the house in order to salvage an agreement with an orang-utan wrangler. Or no, not the post-coital talk: this part had actually come mid-coitus. They'd had a lull during which Wade had reiterated what appeared to have been an earlier attempt to persuade Chloe to go to Indonesia with him. She'd told him, with all too evident reluctance, that it was impossible, and the renewed sense of imminent separation had started them up again. 'Don't come,' she'd said as Wade's groans began to indicate critical levels of excitement.

'Say something unsexy then,' he'd muttered.

'Okay. Tell me what you thought about Charlie's cousin.'

So that Matthew had been compelled to hear himself discussed, this time without the refuge of gaps in the conversation by way of intermittent relief. He could feel the exchange in its entirety now, pressing at him, urging him to replay it like some elaborate injury one has to relive over and over until its power to hurt runs out.

'Well, he's a short guy,' had been Wade's first observation.

'You said. You're a fat guy. He can't help it, you can – so what's your point?'

'That's my point, sugar. I could lose weight if I wanted to, but he'll never gain height. That is a big old difference, not of degree, but of ontology –'

'Oh, stop it. Anyway, he isn't that short.'

'No, but –'

'You didn't think there was something strange about him?'

'Not that I could tell just from looking at him.'

'I think there's something deeply strange about him.'

'You mean he has the hots for you? I wouldn't call that strange, sugar.'

Wade had re-enveloped her in his arms at that point, face against the back of her neck, his large hand reaching around to her breasts. She'd snuggled back against him.

'No, that doesn't bother me. Or it never used to. Now I'm not sure . . .'

'He's getting more serious?'

'It's almost as if he's becoming possessive. As if he thinks we're in an actual relationship. He's started questioning me – asking where I've been, where I'm going. Also . . . Mmm.'

His other hand was moving between her legs and she broke off, given over to some large wave of pleasure.

'Also?'

She'd had to bite her lower lip, hard, before she could control her voice enough to answer.

'He's been acting weird with Charlie,' she said as the sensation ebbed sufficiently for her to speak. 'Needling him . . .'

'Oh, yeah?'

'I mean, I haven't seen it myself but I doubt Charlie's imagining it. Charlie doesn't tend to imagine things.'

'Needling him how?'

'He keeps making these insinuations . . .'

'About?'

'Me.'

'What about you?'

'That I'm being unfaithful.'

'Well, you are, sugar. You are being unfaithful.'

'But he doesn't know.'

'You're sure about that?'

'I'm careful, Wade.'

'So why's he doing it?'

'I think he's deliberately trying to make Charlie suffer. He knows Charlie has a tendency to get jealous.'

'But why would he want to make him suffer?'

'I don't know.'

'Well, I wouldn't worry about it. Not like there's anything you can do about it. Right?'

'But it's so cruel. I mean, towards Charlie.'

'You're awfully considerate of your husband.'

'I love him.'

The words, so unexpected in the circumstances, had shocked Matthew. Her ability to confound him never seemed to exhaust itself. Wade too had seemed surprised.

'You love him?' he'd said, heaving his bulk above Chloe and moving more concertedly. Her phrase had seemed to drive the two of them into suddenly more intense realms of mutual desire.

'You know I love him.'

'You love his dough, I know that.'

'Maybe, but I love him too.'

'More'n you'd love me? If I was that rich? *When* I'm that rich?'

'More than I'll ever love you, Wade.'

'Jesus, you are the most . . . unfathomable . . . human being . . . I have ever . . .'

'Don't come.'

'Met. And I grew up around Catholics.'

157

'That has nothing to do with it. Anyway, there's something else.'

'About you and Charlie?'

'No, about him. Matthew.'

And Matthew had braced himself for another blow, but as it turned out neither Chloe nor Wade were able to distract themselves from the business in hand any longer and for the next several minutes the only sounds inside the little A-frame were moans of pleasure and the occasional protest from a piece of furniture subjected to forces it hadn't been designed to withstand. Time had seemed to thicken then; the seconds growing sticky as clay. He'd forced himself to think of dates of battles, variant recipes for choux pastry, passages from Pascal. *Two errors*, he'd remembered: *1. To take everything literally, 2. To take everything spiritually.* Which of the two am I falling into, he'd wondered, contemplating the scene below where Wade had just enthroned himself in the armchair and Chloe was kneeling down between his sprawled legs, positioning herself with a votive grace that reminded him of one of her butterflies as it settled on the stamen of some garish flower, slowly folding its wings; or again, as they'd moved and her face had reappeared through the next gap in the palings, cushioned sideways on the love seat with a look of rapture as she lay over its arm? Was there an erroneous sense in which this was literal? A true sense in which it was purely spiritual? Turning, she had reached up and drawn Wade down onto the floor below her, in turn lowering herself onto him with a cry of joy. *There are perfections in*

nature to show that she is the image of God and imper-
fections to show that she is no more than his image. That
was one his father had marked and that he, with child-
ishly pleasurable irrationality, had written *No!* next to,
happily aware that nobody except his ghostly co-custo-
dian of this mystic text could possibly have any idea
what he meant.

They'd lain in silence for several minutes afterwards,
Chloe's head on Wade's chest as she idly fondled his
detumescing member and ate a piece of chocolate,
Wade's eyes gazing upward, scanning the ceiling, the
skylight, the carved wooden slats on the balustrade. For
a terrifying moment it had seemed to Matthew the man
had caught the glint of his eye in the candlelit darkness
and was staring straight at him, trying to make sense of
what he was seeing. The prospect of what would happen
if he did had been so far beyond intolerable that Matthew
could only think of it in terms of annihilation. Possibly
in some court of ultimate, celestial arbitration his presence here would be found at least partly understandable,
even partly creditable. (Was he not in some sense acting
on Charlie's behalf?) Certainly, mitigating factors would
be given their due. But no earthly judgement would get
beyond the point of pure outraged horror. And there
would be no mercy. He was well aware of that. No
mercy at all.

Wade's glance travelled on. But as if some unconscious
agency had registered what his eye had failed to discern,
he said:

'You were saying, sugar, about your friend.'

159

'I'm afraid of him,' Chloe had murmured. 'That's why I wanted you to see him. He scares me.'

'Ah, c'mon, sugar. Why?'

'I don't know.'

'I'll tell you what I think, sugar. I think you're mixing up your own guilt about Charlie with the little dude's fixation on you, that's what I think.'

'I don't feel any guilt.'

'My point precisely,' Wade had answered with a chuckle.

Chloe had stood up then, and begun getting dressed.

'He's blackmailing Charlie,' she'd said matter-of-factly.

'*What?*'

Wade's astonishment was almost as great as Matthew's own. At first Matthew thought she was joking or exaggerating for effect, but as she spoke on, it became apparent that she really did think he'd been blackmailing Charlie! He didn't know whether to weep or laugh at the absurdity of it. As he'd listened to the strange warpings and distortions of reality that made up her tale, the urge to interrupt and proclaim his innocence, to stand up on the gallery and shout out the truth, had been almost overwhelming.

Yes, it was true that Charlie had lent him money on and off over the years since his arrival in the States. Yes, it was thanks to Charlie's generosity that he had been able to come up with his stake in the farm-to-table restaurant. Yes, it was also true (though he hadn't realised it was quite so obvious) that he'd hoped at some point to interest Charlie in his food truck idea. But he had always made it very clear that he intended to pay Charlie back as soon as he was in a position to, and in any case none of it was a secret, and it certainly wasn't blackmail!

Wade himself had made the obvious objection:

'I mean, how's that blackmail, sugar? There has to be compulsion of some kind to call it blackmail. He'd have to have some kind of *hold* over Charlie . . .'

'He does.'

'What?'

'Charlie's guilt.'

'For what?'

'For having money. For being luckier than him. For his father giving Matthew's father some bad investment advice a million years ago. For being, you know, a banker. For everything!'

'Yeah, but that's not – I mean, at a stretch you could call that moral blackmail but for actual legal blackmail there'd have to be specific information he was threatening to reveal.'

'All right, so call it moral blackmail. To me there's no difference. He's using Charlie's guilt to extort money out of him. He has been for years. Basically, Charlie's been paying his rent since Matthew followed him here to the States, which I imagine he did with precisely that in mind.'

'Seriously? Paying his rent?'

'I've seen the cheques.'

Untrue! Matthew had wanted to shout out. Unfair! There were just three or four months when Charlie covered my rent! And it was all on the record, written down on the ledger along with the other odd sums. And what the hell, he wondered as the scene replayed itself now, had she meant about me following Charlie to the States? Over the trees, as he considered this, came the unmistakable introduction to Jimi Hendrix's 'Hey Joe'. It was a song Matthew happened to know well. There was a couple he used to supply in the early nineties; middle-aged hippies who'd had the track on a mix they played all the time in their Ladbroke Grove bedsit, where they'd insist he shared a smoke with them whenever he visited. Nothing in the mix was really his kind of music but he'd responded to the emotional build of 'Hey Joe' and the stark economy of its tale of jealous passion. The words weren't audible as he listened now but he knew the simple call-and-response lyrics well enough. The gun, the shooting, then that frenzied dream of escape. *Hey Joe,* he heard as if from deep in his own past, *where you gonna run to now?* and from even deeper, saturated in some ancient sense of yearning and sun-dazzled release: *I'm goin' way down south, way down to Mexico . . .*

Another wobbly guitar solo stretched over the town and then 'Hey Joe' gave way to the screeching bombardment of 'The Star-Spangled Banner'. There was a dim roar from the crowd and suddenly the blackness framed by the skylight above Matthew's head exploded in gold and emerald starbursts with a blast that made the windows rattle.

Grollier was still in the house.

He was in a bathrobe now, sitting on the love seat again, with a beer and a lump of cold beef on a cutting board. Apparently he'd decided not to go to the fireworks after all.

162

Matthew gazed down on him with a sort of despairing indignation. Absurd as he knew it to be, he felt personally cheated by this change of heart; as if he'd been deliberately double-crossed. The man had good as given his word that he was going to the display, hadn't he? But instead here he was carving himself slices of cold beef, thick as carpet samples, and gobbling them down on crackers in between chugging at a beer!

Whatever perverse appeal it had possessed earlier, the idea of being trapped here all night had lost every trace of it, now that it appeared to have become a real possibility. It was so appalling, in fact, that it was almost a relief to have Chloe's bizarre allegations to think about instead.

'Anyway, there *is* something specific,' she'd said, buttoning her blouse.

'Oh, yeah?'

'Charlie had some things happen at Morgan Stanley, which he naively told Matthew about, back in the days when he still thought of him as someone he could confide in.'

'What things?'

'Oh, nothing he could get in trouble for at this point, but not the kind of thing you'd want spread around, and Matthew's apparently aware of that. When we had those English people over the other night they were talking about the financial meltdown and making insinuations about Charlie's career, and Matthew started leaning towards Charlie in this very overt way as if he was trying to remind him he had it in his power to make him extremely uncomfortable at that moment if he wanted to. I didn't take it in at the time, but when Charlie told me about it later I realised I'd seen exactly what he was describing. It was very deliberate, and it was menacing. He was threatening Charlie.'

'Hm.'

'What do you mean, "Hm"?'

'That's still not a real *hold*. I mean, if Charlie can't get in actual trouble for whatever he did.'

'So what are you saying?'

'I'm saying, sugar, that for Charlie to be guilty enough to pay the guy's rent for him, he'd had to have something besides routine rich-boy guilt on his conscience. Else it just doesn't add up. There'd have to be some kind of genuine act of darkness on Charlie's part.'

'No. Not possible.'

'Well then, I'm flummoxed.'

'Charlie's too decent for his own good. That's actually the problem. He has an overdeveloped conscience.'

A smile flared on Matthew's face as he recalled these words. Certain secrets, he had learned, came into the world with a curious immunity to being divulged. Like well-armed viruses, they gave off invincible reasons for being preserved intact at every moment of possible violation. The irony that, if he could somehow convey the truth to Chloe, all it would do would be to confirm her view of him as a blackmailer, was merely a further manifestation of this quality. All kinds of bitter ironies, as a matter of fact, seemed to have begun proliferating around him. That her apparent fear of him, unfounded as it was, would have seemed fully justified, indeed insufficiently urgent, if she'd had any idea where he was at the very moment she was describing it – was one. That the accusation of obsessive behaviour she had gone on to make ('forever loitering around our house in Cobble Hill', was how she'd put it) – had come to acquire an accidental semblance of validity in recent days, was another . . . The litany of accusations unfurled again in his mind. 'Needling Charlie' (how could Charlie have possibly misunderstood him so badly?); blackmailing him, for Christ's sake! Mooching, stalking, other assertions even more bizarre . . . 'I think he wants to move into our home up here,' she'd said at one point, 'take over the guest house or something.' It was as if she'd somehow tuned in to his innocent appreciation of the little cabin, and out of some incomprehensible hostility inflated it into a charge of sinister covetousness . . .

The existence of this hostility, so out of character in the Chloe he thought he knew, was as startling to discover as it was painful. What had caused it? How had she managed to conceal it from him so perfectly, and for so long? Why bother with all the smiles and gentleness; all those tender conversations they used to have, those protestations of interest, affection, concern? Why, if she hated him?

And yet that hadn't been the end of it either. If it had, it might have been easier for him to manage. He could have told himself she was simply two-faced; a hypocrite in whom a dissembling graciousness had become habit, no doubt from having spent too many years looking out at the world from the plinth of Charlie's riches . . . But there had been more to it, and of a nature so unexpected it had left him more bewildered than ever; more pierced and shattered, and – strangest of all – more in love.

'You really do not like this character, do you?' Wade had said.

Chloe had paused then, her face stilling as if the question had sent her unexpectedly inward. After a moment she'd replied quietly:

'I do like him, actually. In some ways I feel very close to him. That's partly why I'm so confused. There's some kind of strange connection between us. I've always felt that. I often have dreams about him, not sexual but intimate. As if we'd known each other in another life. It makes me want to help him.'

'Really? Because he sounds kind of irredeemable the way you describe him.'

Chloe grinned.

'Nobody's irredeemable, Wade, not even you.'

Grollier had laughed.

'You're a piece of work, sugar. You really are.'

'I'll see you in a week,' she'd said, leaning down to kiss him goodbye.

At the door she'd turned back.

'By the way, you forgot to lock up before.'

'I did?'

'You should be careful. There are some sketchy characters in town. Every summer there's a break-in somewhere. Bye, Wade.'

'Bye, sugar. I'll miss you.'

'I'll miss you too.'

*   *   *

Meatspace, he thought now. It had been like a forcible induction into the meatspace of the real.

Wade blew out the candles and carried his dishes into the kitchen, dumping them with a clatter in the sink and then noisily urinating in the bathroom. After that he slid the bolt on the back door open and shut again, returned to the darkened living room to lock the front door, and finally retired into the bedroom. The bedroom light snapped off and after a creak or two of bedsprings there were no further indications of movement.

Meatspace . . . Or not an induction, exactly, since it had left Matthew more confirmed than ever in his wariness of that particular realm. But a vision of it at its most vividly carnal, glistening with the redness of betrayed intimacy, of deep bonds being torn asunder, every fibre bleeding.

Outside, the fireworks were going off in steady succession. He could see them through the skylight: white chrysanthemums flaring blue at their tips, sequinned purses spilling golden coins, the slam of each explosion reverberating off the mountains.

Meatspace . . . And yet even in the midst of it, to have heard her affirm precisely the most hoped-for, uncertain, purely speculative of those bonds; the ones linking her not to Charlie but to himself! *As if we'd known each other in another life* . . . The words rose in his agitated spirit once again like some immensely soothing substance. He was right. He hadn't been imagining things. There was something real, objective, fuelling the compulsions that had drawn him into this strange situation.

The thought, however, intoxicating as it was, brought him back to the more prosaic question of how he was going to get himself *out* of this strange situation. He'd realised at this point that whatever difficulties might be entailed in leaving while Wade was still in the house, it was not going to be possible to spend the whole night crouched up here in the loft. For one thing his bladder was already uncomfortably full and it was inconceivable that he was going to be able to delay emptying it until the morning. For another, the boards creaked, and sooner or later Wade was going to hear something.

His first thought was to wait till the small hours, when Wade could be presumed fast asleep, then scramble down the ladder, unlock the front door, and run. Even with the noisy boards, it seemed a reasonably safe plan. It was no distance from the ladder to the door, which would take only a second or two to unlock. Even if Wade did wake up, there'd be time to disappear into the shadows of Veery Road before he got to the door.

But as Matthew started focusing on the details, dangers he hadn't considered began to present themselves. What if Wade called the cops, or tried to rouse the neighbourhood? The fireworks would be long over by then, and there'd be no crowds in which to lose himself. By the same token he wouldn't be able to drive off unnoticed even if he made it to the truck. No: better to get out while people were still around.

The explosions of the fireworks, which were coming thick and fast now, merged with their own echoes to form a continuous roaring. The display must have been approaching its climax. This was the moment to do it. Immediately, without giving himself a chance to reconsider, he unfolded his stiffened limbs and let himself down the ladder. The living room was almost pitch dark, but he'd seen the ledge where he'd placed the key. He found the ledge without difficulty, and ran his hand along it. But there was no key there. He checked the floor below – maybe it had fallen after Chloe picked it up – but it wasn't there either. Wade must have put it somewhere else when he locked up, or else taken it with him into the bedroom. He'd have to leave through the back door instead. Restraining an impulse to run, he crept quietly towards the rear of the house. Bursts of blue light in the sky gave a flickering glimpse of the back door and he was able to position his hand directly on the bolt without fumbling for it. He slid it back and grabbed the door handle. But the handle wouldn't turn. He tried again, twisting as hard as he could: to no avail. In the next flash of blue he saw that the round black knob had its own small keyhole at the centre. For a few seconds of panicked alertness he searched frantically for a key – over the door frame, under the doormat, behind the sink. He was groping along the counter when he heard a voice directly behind him:

'Mister, I have a gun pointed at you. Don't move.'

He closed his eyes.

'Don't move, okay? I see you move, I'm going to have to shoot you. You got that? You can nod your head.'

Matthew nodded. He felt oddly unafraid, calm almost, as though experiencing some peculiar natural law whereby fear diminished in proportion to the close-ness of its object, vanishing entirely at the point of convergence.

'Now. You're going to hear me look for my phone, which should take all of about four seconds, and then call the police, but I'll be pointing my weapon at you while I do that and I will shoot you if you move a muscle. It's a semi-automatic Ruger, just so you know, single action, so really, don't make any kind of a move. Okay?'

Matthew nodded again, but less in acknowledgement of Grollier's question this time, than of his own sense of what was going to happen. It didn't frighten him at all. In a way, it was a relief. He thought – such was the strange lucidity inside him – of the words from his father's Pascal: *All men seek happiness. This is the motive of every act of every man, including those who go and hang themselves.* He'd often dreamed of being placed in a situation where survival was simply not an option; where the small part of him still obstinately clinging to the little knot of pain and unhappiness that made up most of his existence would finally have no choice but to defer to the other, larger part, that craved only oblivion. It seemed very clear that he was there at last. Only a little courage was required.

Slowly, conscious of having long ago brought to mind every argument in favour and every objection against, he began turning towards his executioner. 'Mister, I told you,' he heard, 'do not fucking move!'

There was something unexpected in the tone; an aggrieved, almost querulous note. On completing the turn, Matthew saw why. Wade, who was naked again, had been bluffing. His hand was empty.

The two of them peered at each other in the flickering blackness for several seconds.

'You!' Wade cried out in startled recognition. His large head turned back to glance into the living room and up toward the loft. Facing Matthew again he hurled himself forward, his bulky figure moving with stunning agility, hands outspread, his fingers braced as if to grab Matthew's throat and throttle him.

Ten

Cooler weather blew in that night. For the first
time all summer, Matthew needed extra blankets
from the cedar chest. Under their comforting
weight he fell quickly asleep. In the morning the day
was blue and clear, and the trees were sparkling. Locking
the guest-house door, he went down for breakfast.

Chloe and Charlie were at the stone table. They looked
scrubbed and cheerful, both of them taking advantage
of the lower temperature to sport new outfits. Charlie
had on a seersucker suit with rolled-up sleeves. Chloe
wore a leaf-patterned dress under a thin silky cardigan.

She took off her sunglasses and grinned at Matthew.

'You didn't wait up for me!'

'Ah, no, sorry. I was tired.'

'How was your night?'

He reached for the coffee pot.

'Uneventful.'

Charlie glanced up from his iPad:

'No luck at the Millstream?'

'I told Charlie I'd sent you on a mission,' Chloe said.

'No.'

'That's too bad,' Charlie said. 'The bar there's supposed to be pickup central.'

'Well, I didn't see any action,' Matthew answered, pouring coffee into his cup. His hand was remarkably steady. 'How were your evenings?'

'Mine was nice,' Chloe said. 'I like seeing Jana on her own. I'm not crazy about Bill.'

'The guy's an asshole,' Charlie said, tapping on his screen. 'He's a reactionary who thinks he's a progressive, which is the worst kind of reactionary.'

There was a box of pastries from Early-to-Bread on the table. Someone must have driven into town.

'What about your evening, Charlie?' Matthew said.

'Exhausting. I didn't get in till almost two.'

'He fell asleep on the Thruway!' Chloe said, putting her hand on Charlie's arm.

'I didn't fall asleep. I very responsibly pulled over and took a nap.'

Charlie yawned, looking at his watch.

'And now we have to hit the road again, right, Chlo?'

'Soon. By the way, Matt, we'll be out for dinner tonight. Lily's in a performance and it'll probably run late.'

'Okay.'

He'd forgotten they were picking up their daughter from camp today.

He reached for a muffin from the cake box.

'How was town?' he asked casually.

174

Chloe shrugged.

'The usual.'

They left after breakfast. As soon as they were gone, he got into the truck and drove into Aurelia, crossing the Millstream bridge and crawling slowly past the Veery Road intersection without making the turn. A man was trimming his hedge on a ladder and a couple of kids were biking around a front yard. Otherwise nothing was going on at that end. He circled back and checked from the County Road end: also quiet. This time he made the turn and drove past the house itself. Nothing: just the LeBaron waiting in the driveway and the silent house jutting above the hedges.

Back at the bridge he parked and climbed down to the creek. Despite the drop in temperature, people were out on the rocks. He made his way downstream until he came level with the back of the A-frame. Summoning the air of a harmlessly inquisitive wanderer, he scrambled up the bank opposite, which sloped up to the fence of a building supply yard. Walking alongside it, he allowed himself a few quick glances across to the other side. Nothing. The back door was closed; the glass squares in its top half reflecting blackly. The small trees flanking the path, sentinel-like presences in last night's darkness, turned out to be dwarf pear trees, laden with small green fruit. A faux-bronze Buddha, Aurelia's ubiquitous totem, sat in the shade of a maple, smiling. The peacefulness of the place was a little uncanny. There ought to have been some outward sign of disturbance, he felt, if only visible to himself; a crack in that trim clapboard exterior, a crooked glint in a window. But the house seemed entirely calm.

He moved on, climbing back down to the water a hundred yards further along, where, for the benefit of anyone watching, he dabbled his feet in a pool, before turning back.

A group of Rainbows had taken possession of a rock near the bridge. One was strumming a small guitar; others had drums and tambourines. A guy with a coiled topknot was sharing a sandwich with a lean grey dog. Torssen was there, Mr 99%, sitting off to one side with the two girls Matthew had met with Pike. He was talking, while the girls listened in silence. One of them lay with her head resting on his thigh. The other, the kittenish-faced one, was on her stomach with her head propped on her hands. Her green hair, to which she had added tints of violet and orange, stuck up in a soft thick tangle and Torssen was absently plying his fingers through it as he spoke.

Matthew stared, wondering again what it was about the guy that provoked such hostility in him. Was it just his own jaundiced distrust of any attitude that divided the world into oppressors and the oppressed, when the only valid distinction as far as he was concerned was between oppressors and, as he put it to himself, 'oppressors-in-waiting'? Or was there something more primitive and personal going on? It occurred to him, as he probed the feeling, that there was probably an element of envy in it; that this figure holding court from the throne-room of his own body, with his jesters and musicians and nubile consorts arrayed about him, might, in some sense, have been himself, had circumstances beyond his control not intervened. Not that this particular image of fulfilment had a monopoly on his capacity for envy; far from it. Depending on his mood, almost any image of success or even just average functionality had the potential to initiate a kind of looping self-interrogation; the abject sense of being confronted by some viable version of himself provoking the question of why he couldn't become that version, which in turn would arouse the fleetingly hopeful sense that all it would take would be a determined act of self-adjustment, followed, however, almost immediately, by the recollection that this adjustment would have to take place in that tantalising stretch of time we wander in so freely and yet can no longer alter in even the minutest degree, namely the past. Which brought him back, like some infernal mobius strip of thought, to that condition of abject susceptibility to the lives of others . . .

Still, it was true that some of those lives had more obvious resonance with his own, which no doubt boosted their power over him, and this man Torssen's was certainly one of those.

One of the girls passed Torssen a small bag and he rolled a joint, executing the ritual with the solemnity of a priest preparing a sacrament. The group smoked it openly, and the smell drifted down to Matthew on the breeze. Good stuff, he noted, remembering the tailings of dusty foliage, half oregano, he used to sell in London. Rudy, his old supplier, impinged on his thoughts, and Rudy's wife Joan. He frowned, shutting them out, and moved on.

Back at the house, he went straight to his room and slid his suitcase out from under the bed, unzipping the lid. Inside, exactly as he had left it last night, was the plastic shopping bag he'd taken from the A-frame's kitchen, bulging with its clutter. He peered in. There was the TAG Heuer wristwatch, the iPhone, the little cheap TracFone, the laptop, the bulging wallet, the Sabatier knife. All present and correct. No reason why it shouldn't have been, of course, but the need to check had been sharply urgent. He closed the lid again, slid the suitcase back under the bed and left.

In the kitchen he cooked himself an omelette of duck eggs and aged Gruyère with some leftover Romesco sauce that needed eating. He was famished, but after a couple of bites he felt abruptly nauseous and tipped the rest into Fu's bowl. Fu, who had a sixth sense for any action involving his bowl, came waddling in immediately, and guzzled the whole mess down.

What now? Swim? Walk? Read? Think more about this hamstrung existence of his? The latter activity had become a little beside the point, he realised. He supposed he should try to take stock of the immediate situation; start processing what had happened and preparing himself for what was to come. But it was hard to get any lasting purchase on it. Thinking about it was like trying to handle a blob of mercury that broke into slithering beads as you touched it. It was like trying to take stock of a dream, or some strange hallucination.

He'd drifted into the living room, and was sitting on one of the rawhide sofas. George's words came back to him from the time they'd talked in the kitchen. Absently, he dug a hand down behind the rawhide seat. Almost immediately he found an iPod mini. For the next several minutes he distracted himself with a methodical search of the deep, faintly oily crevices of the two sofas. By the time he was finished he'd found several Scrabble letters, close to forty dollars in change and bills, and a gold-and-quartz Montblanc fountain pen. He considered leaving it all on the kitchen table for Charlie and Chloe to find when they got back with their daughter, with a note explaining where he'd discovered it, but realised this would raise the question of why he'd been poking around in their sofa in the first place. Mildly amused by the predicament, he stuffed the whole lot back down into the crack. For a moment he felt rather noble and honourable doing this. But then he felt hypocritical, as though it had just been an act for the benefit of some invisible observer, and he dug it out again, all but the Scrabble pieces. Why pretend he was anything other than he was, he thought: a teenage delinquent turned fully fledged adult criminal? In which case he might as well start acting like one.

The atmosphere of those grubby, forlorn years came back to him; aged fourteen to seventeen, running his little business with his scales and baggies out of the tiny bedroom in the West Kensington flat he'd moved into with his mother and sister. One incident in particular asserted itself through the drift of memory. It wasn't an incident he thought about often: it was so bizarre it had a quality of having happened to a third party, and when he did think of it, he could hardly connect it to himself. Dr McCubbin would no doubt have been highly interested in it, but he hadn't discussed it with McCubbin: not because he was embarrassed, but because even by then it had already sealed itself off from him, existing more as an article of faith than a living memory.

He'd gone to the flat of his supplier, Rudy, in Hounslow. Rudy had apparently forgotten he was coming and didn't have the goods, which he kept in a garage in Hatton Cross. He'd told Matthew to wait while he fetched them, saying he'd be back in an hour. Joan, his wife, offered Matthew a cup of tea. She was a gaunt woman with long, platinum-white hair and white-polished fingernails. The two of them sat together at the kitchen table with its porcelain donkey centrepiece, in the panniers of which sat little glass cruets of condiments.

They hadn't been alone before and didn't have much to say to each other. Joan asked about his school and he told her about his crammer in Holborn. They discussed the unusually sunny weather. A silence descended on them. Then Joan looked at him – he never forgot the placid calm in her pale blue, crow's-footed eyes – and said: 'Would you like to fuck me, Matthew?' He was startled and yet the words immediately acquired a kind of fatefulness, as if in some part of himself he had long been expecting them. He remembered walking down a corridor behind her, his forefinger linked with hers, thinking: 'So this is how it's going to happen.' In the bedroom she took off her top and went to the far side of the bed, kneeling on the gold-brown carpet in her bra and skirt. She lit a menthol cigarette. He hesitated in the doorway, unsure what he was supposed to do. There was a mirror etched with Betty Boop on one wall and paintings of a woodland scene in each of the four seasons on another. In the corner was a built-in white closet. 'Come here,' she said. He went over and she unzipped his fly, taking him in her mouth and putting his hands on her breasts, holding her cigarette off to the side. When he was hard she took off her skirt and bra and lay on the bed. 'Is this your first time?' she asked. He nodded. She stubbed out her cigarette and raised her knees. 'Take off my panties.' He remembered the thinness of her thighs as he slid her underwear down; the scant black wisps of her pubic hair. He remembered trying to kiss her as he lowered himself onto her, and the abruptness with which she turned her head away, muttering: 'None of that.' She brought him into her and they went at it missionary style for a bit. 'Very nice,' she said, and then turned over, lighting another cigarette and thrusting her thin behind at him. 'Now hit me. Smack me.' Bewildered – at fifteen he was very innocent in these matters – he gave her a tentative smack. 'Go on, I like it,' she told him. 'Harder. Harder.' After a while she said: 'Now do me again. Put it in.'

Rudy was in the kitchen when they went back, sitting at the table with another man, a soft-looking guy in his forties, with an unshaven double chin. It was this part of the experience that was so strange: so charged and yet so blank. Everyone acted as if nothing out of the ordinary had occurred. Nobody asked where he and Joan had been or what they'd been doing. Rudy introduced the other man to Matthew as his new business partner, Don, who'd given him a lift back from Hatton Cross. Joan put the kettle on and made another cup of tea while Rudy weighed out the grass and hash and counted off the acid tabs, and Matthew paid him.

That was all, and nothing ever happened with Joan again. But a peculiar feeling had lingered with Matthew as he left, a sort of confused dread, and for a long time his mind had gone compulsively back over the experience, itemising every detail, and often recapturing small objects or words he'd overlooked before, but always sensing there was still some large thing that he'd missed.

Later, in his twenties, he'd surmised that Rudy and possibly the other man had been watching through the closet keyhole or some hidden hole in the wall, or maybe through the Betty Boop mirror. Still later, he'd recalled an earlier visit where he'd gone into the room they called the lounge, and had seen, without taking any particular notice of it, a home movie projector on the cocktail cabinet, and it occurred to him that he'd possibly been filmed. But oddly enough even when he interpolated these conjectures back into the memory, they did nothing to diminish its aura of mystery, or reduce the sense of vague dread it still aroused in him.

It was only recently, a year or so ago, that he'd remembered the last part of it, or what he hoped was the last part of it. Without any obvious trigger it had come to him one morning in New York, that Joan had also told him to burn her with the lighted cigarette, and that he had done it: stabbed the red ember, in response to her gasped commands, against her scarred white buttocks. It had seemed a momentous new fact to have discovered, or rediscovered, about himself, full of potential illumination. And yet it, too, had proved oddly enigmatic, yielding little usable self-knowledge, and adding to his confusion.

Only now, for the first time, did it occur to him that its real meaning might be less in the nature of illumination than of prophecy. For was it not, in its masque-like way, a foretelling of last night's culminating gesture: the same hand, a quarter-century older, thrust out in an almost identical motion, the same bewildered shock at the unexpected weapon in its grasp, as though Joan had reached down through time and placed it there; the same sense of irresistible necessity drawing from him an act of violence as savage and surprising to him as if he had been given a lightning bolt to wield?

He took the spoils from the sofa back up to the guest house and put them in the suitcase with Grollier's things. The suitcase had seemed the safest hiding place for the moment. Nobody was going to stumble on its contents by accident. He'd be in New York in a few days, assuming his luck held (though 'luck' didn't seem quite the word), and there'd be plenty of places to get rid of everything. The Montblanc pen he could sell when the time was right, along with Grollier's watch. The rest could be bagged and dumped in trashcans across the city, or thrown in the river.

He swam laps for an hour before going to bed that night, forcing himself up and down the length of the pool. Shivering, he ran up to the guest house and took a long, hot shower. There was a moment, as he lay in darkness, in which he could feel the proximity of tumultuous thoughts that, if engaged, would almost certainly rule out any possibility of sleep. But he'd managed to exhaust himself sufficiently that fatigue soon got the better of him, and he was asleep by the time Charlie and Chloe got back from Connecticut with their daughter.

A child's voice singing a Lady Gaga song rang out from the kitchen as he went down for breakfast the next morning.

Lily had been at music camp. She played the violin and clarinet, and mimicked a range of English and American pop divas uncannily well, complete with cheeky glottal stops and tremulous melisma. When she wasn't making music, however, she was a quiet, watchful girl, with something of Charlie's distrustful air, as if she thought you might be trying to get something out of her.

She broke off the song as Matthew came in, and gave him a friendly, if somewhat impersonal, greeting. He kissed her on the forehead and realised he should have brought a present for her. At one time she'd treated him as a family member, unselfconsciously jumping onto his lap with a book for him to read to her, but in the past couple of years she'd become more reserved.

'How was camp?' he asked.

'It was good.'

'That camp is something else,' Chloe said. 'The show they put on was like Broadway and the Lincoln Center combined. They even served little tubs of ice cream in the intermission.'

Matthew smiled. 'I've always wondered what I missed out on, not going to camp.'

'You never went to camp?' the girl asked.

'We didn't have camp in England.'

'But it's so much fun!'

'That's probably the reason.'

Chloe laughed and Lily, taking the cue, gave a polite chuckle. That was another thing about her; a habit of doing whatever her mother did: echoing her gestures, acquiescing in her moods and wishes; sometimes with a strange sort of cringeing eagerness, as if she weren't quite certain about her mother's approval. There was no obvious reason for this: Chloe treated her with impeccable kindness and patience, and yet the effect of her daughter's behaviour was to suggest something faintly strained in her own. It was the only aspect of Chloe that Matthew had ever found remotely troubling, and he preferred not to think about it.

The morning passed unremarkably. After breakfast Chloe and Lily went off to a Zumba class. Charlie worked upstairs in his office. Matthew sat on the terrace with his father's Pascal. From time to time he checked for news on his computer, an old Toshiba Netbook with a cracked screen. He'd brought it down because the Wi-Fi only reached the guest house erratically. There was still nothing.

After lunch he joined the family by the pool, lying on a wooden sunbed while Chloe and Lily splashed in the water and Charlie floated around in his inflatable armchair. The citrussy scent of some shrubs that had started flowering for the second time that summer drifted on the breeze. Heat rose from the flagstones edging the pool. He gazed out at the three figures, noting his own calmness, again with that odd, though not disagreeable, feeling of detachment from himself. A fantasy took shape in his mind, in which time stalled in a kind of endlessly looping eddy and all the pleasant sensations of this moment, the warmth and soft sounds and gentle motions, simply burbled on forever like some changeless screen-saver.

But by the late afternoon he was beginning to feel restless again. A part of him wanted this lull to last for ever, but another part of him, he realised, was impatient for it to break. He stood up.

'I should get some things for dinner.'

Chloe looked at him, shading her eyes.

'Can't we make do with what we have in the refrigerator?'

'I need nectarines. I want to make a cobbler.'

'Yummy!' Lily called out. 'I love cobbler!'

'Me too,' Charlie said.

'Yes, but . . . it's late, and Matthew shouldn't—'

'It's no problem,' Matthew interrupted her, opening the gate. 'I like going into town.'

He left before Chloe could make any more objections. His desire to drive by the A-frame was as sharp, suddenly, as it had ever been.

This time a Chevy pickup was parked in the driveway, with a metal trailer attached to it.

Forcing himself to keep driving, Matthew glimpsed a man on a riding-lawnmower in the backyard, sending out plumes of grass.

He parked by the bridge and climbed straight down to the creek. The daylight seemed to be throbbing around him. At the top of the bank opposite the A-frame he found himself staring straight into the eyes of the man on the lawnmower. He raised a hand as if in casual greeting, and the man waved back as he rotated his machine back towards the house. A second man, wearing goggles, was weed-whacking around some shrubs at the corner of the kitchen. He was stepping slowly backwards; moving in the direction of the kitchen door. With an effort, Matthew made himself leave. It was possible that you couldn't actually see into the kitchen through the door unless you stuck your face right up to the glass, but he didn't want to be around to find out.

It was coming, he thought. If not now, then soon. Fear was pushing up through the numbed feeling he'd had for the past two days. It was as though what had occurred was only beginning to become real in his own mind, now that the prospect of other people discovering it was looming closer.

He drank copiously at dinner that night, sensing he was going to have trouble sleeping. By the time he'd finished the dishes he could barely keep his eyes open. In bed, he fell asleep instantly. But an hour later he came lurching awake, his heart pounding. Had it happened yet? An awful certainty that it had, gripped him. He got up and took his Netbook down to the pool, to search online for news. Still nothing. He stood up, intending to go back to bed, but instead found himself sidling around the house and into the truck. If anyone heard him, he thought, he could say he'd been unable to sleep and had gone to listen to the drumming. Town was deserted. From the County Road he turned onto Veery Road. The thin dark triangle of the A-frame reached up like a finger saying *sshhh*. The gardeners' truck and trailer were gone. Only the LeBaron stood in the driveway, its lonely persistence charged with odd pathos now, like that of some helplessly loyal pet. I ought to be relieved, Matthew thought. But if anything the stillness of the place – as though he'd somehow sealed it in time – made him more restless than ever. Parking in the pull-off beyond the bridge, he felt as if there were two of him; a self and a second self, ghostlier and yet seemingly more in control of him than the first, as it replicated every movement he made: two of him climbing down to the stream, picking their way with identical motions from rock to rock among the white combs of falling water and the black pools; two of him climbing the wooden steps up the bank below the A-frame, and stepping silently across the lawn to the windowed back door, aware of the dark forms of the pear trees either side of him, the little Buddha cross-legged under the maple.

Covering the door handle with his shirtsleeve, he turned it and stepped inside, closing the door behind him.

The A/C had been on, but there was a bad smell already: human waste and the odour of spoiling meat. In the darkness he made out Grollier's naked body, slumped against the wall like a heap of pillows with dark stains. As he stepped forward, moonlight coming in from the skylight caught the slits of white in the half-open eyes and he flinched back. All right, he thought, steadying himself. All right. This was why he'd come, wasn't it? To see what he'd done; confirm that he hadn't in fact been dreaming or imagining his long evening at the A-frame. Well, here was his proof: the bearded head slumped on the enormous torso, one arm on the floor, the other bent at the elbow with the hand turned back awkwardly as if caught in the act of batting off a fly, legs kicked out across the passage; the whole body, blood-splotched from the neck down, emanating a sort of confused reproach, like some felled colossus who believed he'd been promised immortality.

He stared on. *You!* the man had shouted, incredulous as he recognised Matthew in the flickering darkness. *You!* – glancing back into the living room and up toward the loft as if suddenly understanding everything, and then lunging forward with his empty hands outspread in front of him. That much Matthew remembered vividly. What happened next was less clear in his mind, and in fact never acquired a stable outline. The firework lights strafing the kitchen in bright flashes that made the intermittent darkness all the more impenetrable, no doubt added to the uncertain nature of the episode. Sometimes he saw himself blindly grabbing the kitchen knife only as Wade came charging towards him. Sometimes he'd taken it deliberately out of the knife block the moment he'd reached the back door, and had been highly conscious of having it in his possession all along. Sometimes it really did seem to have materialised in his grip by magic. As for the stabbing itself, it appeared to have occurred in some purely interstitial realm, outside consciousness and intractable to memory. One moment Wade was charging at him like an enraged ape; the next he was thrashing on the floor with a five-inch Sabatier blade in his throat, blood fountaining out from the severed artery in a copious gush while Matthew staggered back to the wall and stood flattened against it, aware only of a roaring in his ears and the fact that his body was vibrating uncontrollably, as if he were in the process of being sucked into a tornado.

Eleven

A t around five the following afternoon, he went out from the kitchen, where he'd been making focaccia dough, and walked over to the pool. Chloe was lying on a sunbed, wearing earbuds and laughing at something on her phone. She liked listening to comedy podcasts and on those occasions there would be the minor delight of seeing her break into helpless laughter without visible cause.

It was a beautiful afternoon, the light so clear he could see small insects at the far end of the pool, glinting in the air above the water.

'Coming for a swim?' Chloe asked, tapping her phone. She was wearing one of her thin cotton shirts over her swimsuit. Her hair was loosely gathered in a leather clasp, falling in dark strands.

'Thinking of it,' Matthew said. 'I was actually wondering if it was warm enough.'

'I know. It's getting cooler. I think the Monarchs have started leaving.' She gestured over to the butterfly garden where a few desultory specimens were still wandering through the air.

'Where do they go?'

'Mexico.'

'Lucky them!'

She smiled.

'Want to hear something hilarious?'

She held out one of her earbuds, leaving the other in her ear.

'Sure.'

He went over and perched on the end of her sunbed.

'Come closer,' she said. 'It won't reach.'

He slid closer to her and put in the earbud. Chloe said a name that didn't mean anything to him.

'He's an actor but he also does stand-up. This . . . This person I know who goes to a lot of comedy clubs put me onto him.'

She tapped the phone and the comedian's voice came into Matthew's ear. He laughed along with Chloe, but he wasn't listening. To be sitting there, joined to her through the looping white scribble of the earbuds, close enough to feel the warmth of her body, was a novel experience, strangely intimate, and he found himself wanting to take note of every detail of it: her arm in its weightless shirt brushing against him as she laughed; the sunlight on her fine small teeth; her perfume that was like the scent of something grown in paradise; above all the private atmosphere of happiness she dwelt in, that at this proximity was something you could almost touch and taste and see. The intense love he felt for her seemed to dilate and sparkle inside him. He sat motionless, drinking in the unexpected blissfulness of the moment.

It was Charlie who brought it to an end, appearing at the gate in his swimming trunks. He was looking at his iPad.

'Hey, Chlo, didn't we meet Wade Grollier? The director?'

Chloe took out her earbud.

'What?'

Charlie walked in through the gate, still looking at his screen.

'Didn't we meet Wade Grollier?'

Very coolly Chloe said:

'Who?'

'Wade D. Grollier. Movie guy.'

'I don't know.'

'I think we met him at some fundraiser. Big guy with a beard.'

She shrugged.

'Maybe. Why?'

'He was renting a house up here this summer.'

Matthew braced himself.

'Oh,' Chloe said with perfect nonchalance.

'Yeah. He was just killed.'

No sound came from Chloe for a second or two.

'What do you mean?' she said.

'He was found dead in his rental house.'

'What?'

'Stabbed. They found him today.'

'What . . . Where?'

Charlie looked down at his screen. 'Veery Road – that's the one that goes by the creek, isn't it?'

Chloe didn't answer. She had stood up, putting on her sunglasses, and was walking over to Charlie.

'I'm pretty sure we did meet him,' Charlie said as she looked at the screen over his shoulder. 'At that thing in Aspen, where they had the hot-air balloons . . .'

Chloe had turned pale and Matthew could see that her hands were clenched tight.

'Don't you remember? Must have been two, three years ago.'

'Maybe. What else does it say?'

Charlie flicked the screen.

'That's all. It's just a statement from the Sheriff's Department. Found stabbed earlier today . . . Treating it as murder . . . That's his picture.'

'Oh God.'

'Unbelievable, right?'

Chloe moistened her lips, but said nothing.

She detached herself from Charlie and walked to the gate, cradling her elbows. Matthew could feel, almost on his own nerves, the horror surging through her.

'Where are you off to?' Charlie called after her.

'Lily.'

She moved quickly towards the house. After she'd gone, Charlie gave a quiet laugh:

'Psycho on the loose, she's thinking.'

Matthew gave a vague nod. He'd known his reactions were going to have to be very carefully calibrated once the discovery was made, but he could tell already that this was going to be more complicated than he'd imagined. Aside from the need to hide any awareness of how Chloe would surely be feeling under her own, equally necessary, masquerade, it was also going to be crucial not to seem out of step with the casual attitude that Charlie, who had no reason to feel personally affected, would naturally assume.

Charlie continued:

'I doubt that's what it is, though. Probably just some meth-head burglar who wasn't expecting to find anyone home.'

'You think?'

'Yeah, or one of those Rainbow people.'

He plunged into the pool and began swimming laps. Matthew went inside. The TV was on in the upstairs bedroom. He could hear its muffled noise through the kitchen ceiling, under the squeak of Lily's clarinet from along the corridor. There was a radio in the kitchen, but he couldn't find any news on it. He fetched his Netbook from the living room and found a couple of breaking news stories that had the same information Charlie had read from his iPad.

Charlie came in from his swim and joined Chloe upstairs. An hour later the two of them came down for dinner.

'Like I told you, Matt,' Charlie said, 'burglary gone wrong. They had the sheriff on the local news. So we're off the hook for anything creepier. Right, Chlo?'

'Right.' Chloe poured herself a drink.

'What did they say?' Matthew asked, trying to strike a tone of neutral interest.

'Basically just that. Someone broke in thinking he was out, got surprised and stuck a knife in him. The owner of the house found the body this morning but it happened a while ago.'

'They can't tell exactly?'

'I guess that takes some time to determine. Anyhow, according to the owner he was due to fly out to Malaysia the day before yesterday, so—'

'Indonesia,' Chloe corrected him.

'No, I think she said Malaysia.'

She seemed about to insist, but swallowed down her drink instead.

'I'm guessing it happened the night of the fireworks,' Charlie said. 'Everyone in town goes, so it's an obvious time for a break-in.'

'Right.'

'It'll put a damper on the summer rental market, that's for sure.'

Chloe went over to the drinks cabinet. Matthew heard the bottle clinking against her glass but managed to stop himself from looking.

'Sorry, that was a callous thing to say,' Charlie said. 'I guess I'm spooked by the fact that we met the guy. Chloe does remember, by the way, Matt.'

'Oh, yes?'

Matthew looked at Chloe. She nodded.

'What was he like?'

Her eyes met his, and he made himself hold their glance. Her poise impressed him. Aside from the shaky hands and the fact that she was drinking at three times her usual rate, there was little outward indication of what she must have been feeling. Certainly Charlie didn't seem to have any inkling of it.

'Oh, you know . . . It was at one of those events where you chat to hundreds of people. He seemed nice enough . . .'

'Was he . . . Did he have a family?'

'I have no idea.'

'He lived with some actress in Soho,' Charlie said. 'She's off filming in the desert. Apparently he was up here to rewrite the script of his new movie.'

'What actress?' Matthew asked, trying to second-guess what a guiltless version of himself would be saying.

'I forget. Who was it, Chloe?'

'I have no idea,' Chloe said with a brusqueness that made Matthew nervous. He was well aware that his safety depended as much on Chloe's ability to put on a convincing performance as it did on his own.

'But listen,' she said. 'Let's not talk about this right now, shall we? Lily doesn't know and I don't want to scare her.'

'Agreed,' Charlie answered.

The topic wasn't mentioned at dinner, and Chloe went off upstairs immediately after. Matthew cleared up while Charlie and Lily embarked on a game of Scrabble in the living room. When he was finished he looked online for more news. There were tributes from fans and colleagues, but nothing new about the investigation. He went to bed without any serious expectation of being able to sleep, which turned out to be the case, though he drifted off for a couple of hours just as day was breaking and the birds were beginning to sing.

Breakfasting alone he found a report on the murder in the *New York Times* online, along with a short obituary. Neither contained anything he didn't already know. Later that morning Charlie came home from tennis with the *Aurelia Gazette* and the *East Deerfield Citizen*.

'He's all over the *Citizen*,' he said, sprawling down on the sofa.

'Who is?' Chloe asked. She'd been upstairs most of the morning, but had gone outside a little while ago, and had just come back in with some wildflowers, which she was arranging in a vase. She was wearing more eye make-up than usual, Matthew noticed. Other than that, it was hard to tell whether there was any objective basis for the aura of precarious frailty he detected around her, or if he was only noticing it because of what he knew. Lily was up in her room, her voice rising uninhibitedly over the tinny accompaniment of a karaoke machine.

'Wade D. Grollier,' Charlie answered his wife. 'Want to hear what they say?'

Chloe cleared her throat before answering.

'Sure.'

'Not interrupting you, Matt?'

Matthew had found a sudoku book in the bathroom and spent the last couple of hours doing puzzles. Plunging his mind into the realm of pure numbers seemed to give him some relief from his own thoughts, which had begun circling around the variables of what might or might not happen now that the body had been found, and how best to react to each eventuality. This ceaseless but largely pointless activity was what had kept him awake for most of the previous night.

'Of course not,' he said.

'I'll give you the highlights. Let's see. Police unable to pinpoint exact time of death but believe it occurred some time during the Aurelia Volunteers' Day fireworks. So I was right about that . . . Director survived by a sister who issued a statement calling him one of the kindest, funniest, most creative blah blah blah . . . Staying in Aurelia to work on a screenplay . . . Not married but living in New York with girlfriend, actress Rachel Turpin. Right, of course. Spokesperson for Turpin said the actress, who is currently on location in Arizona, was devastated and blah blah . . . Officers from the Sheriff's Department canvassing neighbours on Veery Road and throughout Aurelia for possible leads . . . Case being handled by detectives from Homicide and Burglary divisions . . . Murder weapon believed to be a kitchen knife missing from the house . . . Any information from members of the public blah blah blah . . .'

He tossed the paper aside.

'East Deerfield Burglary division. Now there's a phrase to strike fear into the most hardened criminal's heart! Maybe the guy'll just turn himself in out of sheer terror.' He laughed. It was a quirk of Charlie's to be contemptuous, on principle, towards the police and uniformed officials in general.

'Why are they so sure it was a burglary?' Chloe asked.

'As opposed to what? An assassination? Some rival director jealous of his awards?'

Chloe shrugged.

'I mean, was anything actually stolen?'

'Well . . . Presumably.'

After a moment, Chloe said:

'Does it say what?'

Charlie picked up the paper and scanned the piece again.

'No. But – would it, necessarily?'

'I guess not.'

She adjusted some flowers in her vase, and picked up a photography book. Matthew glanced over, trying to guess what was going through her head. It occurred to him that she might have been thinking about Grollier's disposable TracFone; hoping it had been stolen, perhaps, so that the police wouldn't find her number on it. It was too bad he couldn't tell her he had it safely in his own possession.

Charlie looked at his watch.

'I should get going. Big meeting this afternoon.'

He went up to take a shower. Before long Chloe put aside her book and casually reached for the newspaper. Grollier's face filled most of the front page, broad and smiling. Matthew watched out of the corner of his eye as she looked at the picture, her own face expressionless. After a while she stood up and, without a word, went out through the glass doors. Halfway across the lawn she stumbled on something, almost tripping over, though she moved on as though she hadn't noticed. Passing Charlie's meditation garden, she wandered into the woods at the edge of the property, disappearing behind the grey trunks. She was gone for the rest of the morning.

Lily had been invited to a birthday party that afternoon, for a girl she'd met at camp. To Matthew's surprise, Chloe invited him along for the ride.

'They sound interesting, the parents. You should come.'

'Are you sure? I wouldn't want to gatecrash . . .'

'No. It's just one of those things where they invite the adults to stick around if they want to. I'd drop Lily off but it's all the way over in Klostville. Come, Matt!'

They set off in the Lexus. Chloe hummed quietly as she drove. She seemed dazed, absent, and Matthew wondered if she'd taken a tranquilliser. Lily sat in the back, listening to music on her headphones. Veery Road was cordoned off; the words **'Sheriff's Line Do Not Cross'** running in black letters along the yellow tape. News vans and police vehicles were parked on the County Road verge. Chloe glanced down towards the A-frame as they passed. She didn't say anything but it wasn't hard to imagine what she was feeling. An urge to make some comforting gesture gripped Matthew. He almost felt he could touch her shoulder in silent sympathy without danger, as if there were some point of contact between them that existed outside the practical exigencies

201

of the situation. He restrained himself, however, aware of the danger of giving even the remotest hint of what he knew.

Glancing in the mirror, Chloe said quietly:

'Did you ever see any of his movies?'

For form's sake Matthew thought he should ask whose.

'Wade Grollier's. That was Veery Road back there. Where he was killed.'

'Ah, right. No, I don't think I have. Have you?'

'I've seen every one of them.'

He looked for a tone of ordinary surprise.

'What are they like?'

'I think you'd enjoy them. They're very funny and warm and . . . human. Even though they're full of robots and talking animals!'

He gave a polite laugh. Was this why she'd invited him along? To talk about Grollier? If so, he felt he should do what he could to rise to the occasion.

'You said he was nice, that one time you met him . . .'

She was silent a long moment, and it seemed to him he could feel her struggling with an intense desire to talk, perhaps even to blab out the whole story of her affair.

'We barely spoke,' she said, clearing her throat. 'But he must have made an impression on me. I went out and got hold of all his films.'

'I'd like to see them. Maybe we could watch one tonight . . .'

'Maybe.'

She rummaged in her purse, bringing out a pair of sunglasses that hid half her face. Matthew turned away, doing his best to conceal any awareness of her emotion. In the mirror, he saw Lily take a pair of chequer-framed shades from her backpack and put them on, gazing up at her mother's reflection. Chloe stared at her a moment before smiling. Again there was that slight impression of strain in her relationship with the girl. She started humming again; a light, tuneless sound that seemed designed to keep the world at arm's length. By uncertain processes of thought Matthew found himself remembering Charlie's comment about his first wife's reluctance to have a child: how he'd been afraid it meant she wanted to go on 'fooling around with other guys', and with a little jolt he realised he might have just stumbled on something interesting. Chloe had become pregnant with Lily almost immediately after she and Charlie were married. Charlie had told Matthew the news over the phone, and Matthew had congratulated Chloe the next time he saw her in Cobble Hill. She'd thanked him, but he'd been struck by a distinct lack of enthusiasm for the prospect of impending motherhood. 'It's not exactly what I had planned for this moment in my life,' she'd said, 'but I guess that's the way it goes.' He'd assumed the pregnancy must have been an accident, and that she'd simply decided to make the best of it (his later discovery that she was a practising Catholic had seemed to confirm this). But now, as he considered it in the light of Charlie's comment about Nikki, it seemed to him things might have been more complicated. Had Charlie somehow pressured his new wife into having a child before she was ready? Got her pregnant so as to lock her into the marriage tightly enough to ward off his own jealousies? Not that he'd have forced anything: his benign image of himself wouldn't have allowed that. But he was a good manipulator, Charlie; very proficient at getting what he wanted without seeming to twist your arm. You could say it was a specialty of his, in fact, Matthew thought morosely. If nothing else, he was quite capable of being deliberately careless in bed. And of course, he'd have been able to pretend to argue for terminating the pregnancy (Matthew could hear him doing it; all scrupulous devil's advocacy against himself), knowing full well that Chloe wouldn't consider it . . .

Was that it? he wondered, turning back to her. Was that what had pushed her into Grollier's arms, or at least enabled her to act on her attraction to him? There was nothing vengeful or calculating about her: he was certain of that, but the delicate mechanism of her psyche was such that even if she'd had no idea of having been manipulated, let alone of punishing Charlie for it, the sheer drastic fact of it, lodged in the living tissue of her marriage, was bound to have summoned into existence some equally drastic counter-measure somewhere along the line. In which case poor old Charlie had had it coming . . .

A few miles beyond Klostville, the GPS took them up a steep mountain road and onto a driveway that skirted a grassy meadow. At the end was a wooden house with a stone terrace where several adults and young girls were gathered. Solar panels gleamed on the roof, and an open-sided shed of rough timbers filled with neatly stacked logs stood to one side. There was a fenced chicken coop, and a paddock with a donkey in it and some small goats. A pleasant farmyard smell scented the air; sweetish and mealy.

A tall man in his thirties greeted them on the terrace, introducing himself as Philippe. He spoke with a French accent but his wife, Caitlin, who came over a moment later, seemed thoroughly American; gangly and blonde with a generous laugh.

'So great to meet you,' she said, shaking their hands and looking from one to the other. 'Natalie is very smitten with your daughter.'

She seemed to assume that Matthew was Lily's father, and Chloe made no attempt to correct her. They were introduced to the other adults.

'Do you guys live around here?' a bearded man in a T-shirt asked.

'Aurelia,' Chloe answered. She'd taken off her sunglasses and seemed to be making a determined effort to appear relaxed and cheerful.

'Aurelia!' another guest exclaimed. 'Isn't that where that movie director was just killed?'

'That's right,' Matthew said, answering for Chloe.

The guest, a woman with long silver hair, shook her head:

'Awful! Do the police have any idea who it was?'

'Not as far as we know.'

'Truly awful,' the woman repeated.

Caitlin brought out dips and carrot sticks from the kitchen while Philippe led the girls off on a treasure hunt, piling them into a wagon attached to a small tractor. The dozen-odd adults chatted on the terrace, sampling the dips and drinking craft beers from the cooler. They were a mixture of locals and weekenders. The silver-haired woman was a sculptor. The bearded man worked as a fishing and wilderness guide. There was a chiropractor and a couple who ran a shoe store. It seemed to Matthew that they were all under the impression he was Chloe's partner, and he found himself slipping mentally into the role; sitting close to her, opening her beer, letting his arm brush carelessly against hers. He was oddly relaxed. The individual who had spent the last few weeks in a state of neurotic, spiralling obsession seemed utterly unconnected to him. He felt affable, even charming. It was as if, playing the part of Chloe's lover, he was able to draw on qualities he couldn't access as himself, most notably the sort of easy-going, half-serious curiosity that had always seemed to him the elusive key to getting along with strangers. He found himself in conversation with Caitlin about the enormous flagstones on her terrace. She described how she and Philippe had transported them from a disused quarry on the ridge above their house, using the old quarrymen's technique of building an ice road in winter and sliding the pieces down. Genuinely interested, he questioned her about the house, the animals, their lives here in general. They'd moved from the city three years ago, she told him, where they'd bought and sold houses that had gone into foreclosure. Philippe, a graduate of Wharton as well as some eminent-sounding French institute, still did some real estate, but their aim was to live entirely off the land. 'Homesteading' Caitlin called it, though from the plans she described – building cellars into the hillside for goat cheese, and raising pigs for *charcuterie* in mobile foraging pens through the woods behind the house – it sounded more ambitious than that. She herself had grown up in Manhattan, but her grandparents on both sides were Wisconsin farmers, and as she described her and Philippe's new life, she seemed to radiate a more than purely personal happiness, as though some large and significant destiny were being fulfilled.

After a while she excused herself and went back inside the house. The silver-haired woman and some of the other guests were still talking about Grollier's murder; trading theories about what had happened. Matthew turned towards them, listening in. One of the shoe-store couple had heard that Grollier's body was found naked, and was surmising some kind of sexual assignation gone wrong. The chiropractor seemed to know for a fact that the police were planning a raid on the Rainbow encampment to search for the stolen property. The wilderness guide echoed what Charlie had said:

'I'll bet it was just some drug-addled drifter who's probably halfway across the country by now . . .'

He tuned out. The air was cool, but the sun itself was pleasantly warm. He tipped his face to it, closing his eyes and basking in its intimate heat. A fantasy formed in his mind: living up here in the mountains with Chloe, opening a little restaurant with food from local farmers and 'homesteaders', cultivating a group of friends like these. His visits to the A-frame felt very distant from him. The stabbing itself seemed to have receded to a point of almost imperceptible remoteness.

The little rural fantasy played on in his mind. A funny name for the restaurant occurred to him – Discomfort Food – and he chuckled softly, knowing it would amuse Chloe too. The talk around him had moved on from Grollier and he listened in again as it turned to the price of firewood, the surge in the local bear population, intrigues at the Klostville Town Board . . . There was something appealing about it all; an easy, expansive ordinariness he hadn't encountered for a long time; not in the pinched conditions of his own life and not in the more luxurious spaces of Charlie's either. Charlie's wealth made him guarded, wary of people's motives for befriending him, and he lived a rather solitary life as a consequence. He and Chloe had done almost no entertaining this entire summer. Even the people who were going to be ousting Matthew in a couple of days were, as it turned out, just a potential business partner and his family.

Caitlin came out of the kitchen carrying a tray of plates and glasses.

'They just had a guy from the Sheriff's Department on the radio. The barman at the Millstream Inn remembers seeing Grollier in there the night he was killed. Apparently he got a call from someone and left in a hurry right after. They're putting out an appeal for the caller to come forward.'

Matthew forced himself not to look at Chloe, but he could feel her tighten beside him. The other guests began talking.

'Can't they just track the person down from the guy's call records?'

208

'Maybe his phone was stolen.'

'They'd still be able to get the records though, wouldn't they, from the carrier?'

'Depends what kind of phone it was.'

Half-listening, he tried to gauge the seriousness of the development. Assuming Chloe had called Grollier on his TracFone, and that Grollier had paid for that phone with cash, there was no reason to think the police would trace the call to Chloe. But what if she'd called him on his iPhone? Or what if the disposable phone had been paid for with a credit card and was therefore traceable? Or suppose Chloe decided, regardless, to come forward as the caller? Her good Catholic girl's conscience was apparently flexible enough to permit an affair, but he wasn't so sure it would allow her to obstruct the investigation of a murder.

He turned to her. She was following the conversation with a plausible air of detached curiosity, even putting in the odd comment of her own. But there was a fragility in her bearing, a constriction in her smile, and even if no one else noticed it, he could feel the immense effort of self-control she was making.

She smiled at him – he'd been staring, he realised – and he smiled back, wishing he could beam some strength at her, or at least a sense of how dangerous it would be, for both of them, if she lost her nerve.

Twelve

'There are forty-five million people living in poverty in this country,' Charlie said, reaching for some smoked sturgeon he'd brought back from the city. 'They can't put up collateral for a big loan, but relatively tiny amounts of money can make a huge difference, and the thing is they pay it back! Or at least the *women* do. The women actually have a near-one-hundred per cent repayment rate.'

It had rained in the night; a soft drumming like fingers on a desk, and it was still coming down steadily. Charlie was in a good mood. His deal was coming together, and in his exuberance he seemed to have forgotten his earlier reluctance to discuss it in front of Matthew.

'Interesting,' Chloe said. She seemed composed, if not exactly relaxed.

'Yeah, I think we're going to make micro-loan lending to impoverished women a centrepiece of our strategy.'

'That's excellent, Charlie.'

'It'll take some packaging, to get it across to investors, but it stacks up. It's kind of exciting. We're actually feeling rather proud of ourselves!'

'You should be. Isn't that great, Lily? Did you hear what Daddy said?'

'That's great, Daddy.'

Matthew listened absently, smiling and nodding in the right places though his mind was on other things. As of tomorrow he'd be gone for four days, which seemed a long time not to be able to follow developments first-hand, and this was nagging at him. Chloe's state of mind, in particular, was something he felt he needed to monitor closely and he wasn't going to be able to do that from the city. So far she seemed to have decided it was more important to protect her marriage than help the cops. But that could easily change, and he'd have preferred to be able to see it coming.

Lily wanted to play Scrabble after breakfast. Matthew began to clear the dishes, but Chloe insisted he come and play with them.

'We'll clean up later.'

They went into the living room and set up the board on the coffee table. For a while they played without speaking, lulled by the steady rain into a peaceful silence. Even Matthew was able to relax a little. His mind drifted back to that first game of the summer, when Charlie had been so unamused by his joke word 'SIOUXP'. He found himself thinking of family Scrabble games when Charlie had come to live with them in London: the way he'd been torn between wanting to be a part of the household, and wanting it known that he considered the whole rigmarole to be, in some crucial way, not 'cool'.

'Coolness' had been extremely important to Charlie at fourteen, Matthew remembered. He'd arrived a year late at their school, which made it difficult for him to make his mark, or at least to get the kind of immediate high-status social ranking to which he seemed to feel entitled. Being cool had evidently been something he believed he could turn into a ticket to popularity. He was already somewhat cool, intrinsically, from the other boys' point of view, just by being American, but he took a lot of trouble to finesse it. Matthew had shared a bedroom with him for over a year, so he'd been able to observe the process close up, and it had been a revelation. The Dannecker family had never been remotely interested in fashion or pop culture, but suddenly here was this boy in their home who, to Matthew's admiring astonishment, would spend hours in front of the mirror, gelling his hair, trying on different outfits, with and without Ray-Bans, Discman, Yankees hat, Converse sneakers. Even on schooldays he'd do things with the school suit to sharpen it up. Fancy belts, a pair of cowboy boots he ordered from Arizona . . . But it had been about attitude also, Matthew thought, remembering the subtle sneer fixed permanently on his cousin's hand-some face at that time, and the way he had of rolling his eyes, that made you feel ashamed of whatever crime against coolness you'd just committed. He'd do it when anyone in Matthew's family used one of the pet words they'd held onto from when Matthew and his sister were little – 'polly' for porridge, 'mimi' for milk . . . It was just their way of amusing each other, but Charlie had made the whole family self-conscious about it.

All of which had impressed Matthew deeply. He'd been Charlie's fan from the start. He'd begun imitating him slavishly, which turned out to be a highly effective way of gaining his friendship. Charlie had seemed to enjoy having his younger, smaller acolyte at his side, piloting him across the schoolyard when he first arrived, or showing him how to get around London on the bus and Tube. Matthew had accepted his role as the junior partner unprotestingly, but he'd also felt proprietorial about Charlie. He'd liked showing him off, basking in the reflected glory, though he was also just plain proud of him in himself. He'd heard his sister describe him to a friend on the phone as 'princely' and the word had seemed to sum him up precisely.

'Matt, weren't you at the Millstream bar the night of the fireworks?' Charlie said, jolting Matthew back into the present. He'd been reading on his iPad in between turns.

Matthew answered carefully.

'Yes . . .'

'Like at around seven, seven-thirty?'

'Probably.'

'That guy Grollier was there. The barman remembers seeing him.'

Matthew paused, waiting for Chloe to remind Charlie not to talk about this in front of Lily, but she seemed to have forgotten that useful restraint on Charlie's stubborn interest in the story.

214

'That's right,' Matthew answered. 'It was on the news yesterday. They were talking about it at Lily's party.'

'You must have seen him there yourself.'

'Huh. I hadn't thought of that.'

'Apparently he got a call at the bar around seven-thirty and left in a hurry right after.'

'Right. That's what they said.'

'So you might have seen him talking on his phone.'

Matthew was about to say he'd already left by seven-thirty, but decided to remain vague about the timing of his departure.

'I guess it's possible.'

'Was the bar crowded?'

'Not especially.'

'But you don't remember seeing him?'

'I mean, I don't really know what he looks like.'

'Oh, he's unmistakable. He's a big guy, built like a tank. Kind of a loudmouth too, right, Chlo? You'd definitely know if you saw him. What I'm saying, Matt, is if you remember anything about him, it might be worth letting those people at the Sheriff's Department know. They obviously need all the help they can get.'

Chloe had stood up. For a moment she remained motionless. Then, as if to explain the action, she went into the kitchen, murmuring that she'd be right back.

'You're right,' Matthew said. His mouth had gone very dry.

'Even if it was just whether he was looking happy or upset while he talked.'

'Yes. I'm trying to remember if I saw him.'

'Your turn, Daddy,' Lily said.

Charlie looked at his letters. Chloe came back in from the kitchen with a saucer of kumquats and chocolate. She put her hand gently on Charlie's shoulder.

'Maybe you shouldn't be on your screen while we're playing.'

'Right. Right. Sorry.'

They played on.

A few minutes later the game was interrupted again, this time by the ringing of the front doorbell. It was such a rare occurrence that all four looked at each other, as if unsure what the sound actually was.

Charlie stood up.

'Better not be those Watchtower people.'

'Don't be rude to them if it is,' Chloe called after him.

They heard the door opening and muffled voices. Charlie called back from the kitchen:

'Uh . . . It's the police, Chloe. They want to talk to us about Wade Grollier.'

Chloe was still for a moment; her slight figure seeming to brace itself.

'Go to your room and practise, sweetheart,' she said to Lily.

The girl left obediently. Chloe stood up, her face glassily expressionless, and climbed the three steps to the kitchen level. Matthew, whose first instinct was to absent himself, decided on second thoughts to follow after her.

In the kitchen Charlie motioned at a man in a jacket and tie.

'This is Detective . . .'

'Fernandez,' the man said. 'And my colleague, Officer Lombardi.' He nodded towards a woman in uniform, who was wiping the rain from her face with a handkerchief.

Charlie introduced Chloe and Matthew. The detective shook their hands, wafting a scent of cologne from his jacket.

He looked about forty, with a thick black moustache and tired, dark eyes. The uniformed woman was younger; wide-shouldered and pale, her face a studious blank.

'Apparently we showed up on a list of possible social connections,' Charlie said. He looked back at the detective. 'Through his Facebook contacts, I'm guessing? I notice his name comes up sometimes on those mutual friends notifications.'

The detective nodded vaguely.

'I was just telling your husband, ma'am, we're trying to track down any possible social or business connections of Mr Grollier here in Aurelia.'

The detective's voice, pleasantly soft and sombre, had a faint Hispanic accent. Puerto Rican, Matthew guessed.

'I don't imagine he had many,' Charlie said. 'This isn't exactly celebrity country up here.'

The detective smiled.

'There's actually a lot of folks who turn out to know people he knew. Four degrees of separation, isn't that what they say?'

'Six, I think,' Charlie said. 'Though in our case just one, since we did actually meet him in the flesh.'

'Oh, I thought—'

'Not up here, as I said, but a couple of years ago, at a fundraiser in Aspen. Chloe talked to him a little. I barely said hello, but I remember him. Smart guy, kind of flamboyant.'

'But you definitely didn't run into him here in Aurelia?'

'No, no. We didn't even know he was up here. I wish we had! Maybe things would have turned out different. Who knows, maybe we'd have had him over for dinner that night . . .'

The detective nodded.

'Well, we'd still like to talk to you, if you don't mind. Shouldn't take more than a few minutes.'

'Of course.'

'Let's go in the living room, shall we?' Chloe said, looking at the kitchen table, which was still covered in breakfast things. She turned to lead the way, but then seemed to have a change of heart. 'Or actually—' She began briskly clearing off the kitchen table.

'Chlo,' Charlie said. 'Let's just go in the living room.'

She opened her mouth as if to argue, but didn't.

'Okay.'

There was a peculiar, stricken look in her eyes as she said this.

'Shall I make some coffee?' Matthew asked. It seemed to him he needed an excuse to remain present in the conversation.

'You know what? I wouldn't say no to some coffee,' the detective said. The uniformed officer shook her head.

Matthew made the coffee. When he brought it into the living room, Charlie was telling Fernandez about the Millstream's reputation as a singles scene, which appeared to be news to the detective.

'I'll have to remember to stay away,' he joked, tapping his wedding ring.

Matthew handed him his coffee and sat on an ottoman. Chloe was perched next to him on the edge of one of the sofas. It was clear to Matthew that she was agitated, and he wondered what could be bothering her, beyond the obvious.

'Matt,' Charlie said, 'I was just telling these guys you were there the same time as Grollier.'

'Right.'

'Did you see him?' the detective asked.

'You know, I'm thinking maybe I did. He's . . . He was big, right?'

'Two hundred and twenty pounds, give or take. Beard. Good head of hair.'

'Right. There *was* a rather hefty guy there, though I don't remember seeing him talk on the phone. I'm pretty sure he had a beard. And he was kind of extrovert.'

'Meaning?'

Charlie said:

'Outgoing, uninhibited.'

'No,' the detective said, 'I mean what form did his extrovert behaviour take?'

'Well, he talked a lot.'

'To anyone in particular?'

'Hmm.' Matthew frowned as if trying to remember. He needed a moment to calculate how much he could safely tell the detective. His instinct had been to say as little as possible, but it occurred to him the barman would have already described the scene, so there was probably little to be gained from holding back, and he certainly didn't want to risk seeming evasive.

'Well, he was asking about the fireworks, and people were telling him how great they always were.'

'Did you hear him invite anyone to go along with him?'

The barman must have said something about the 'posse'.

'Yes, I think he *was* trying to get people to go with him. I don't know how seriously . . .'

'Did he ask you?'

'Me? No, but I was on my way out by then.'

'Why was that?'

'No reason. I mean, there was no one there that particularly interested me.'

'So to speak,' Charlie said with a chuckle.

'So you left?'

'Yes.'

'How long had you been there?'

'Maybe forty-five minutes?' It had been more like twenty, but he thought that would seem oddly short. 'But you know, I think when I left he *was* actually talking to one person in particular, a woman.'

Fernandez waited for him to continue.

'She had a book, I think. He was asking her about it.'

'Could you describe her?'

'Youngish – maybe late twenties. Kind of straight mousey hair, down to about her shoulders.'

'Do you remember anything about the book?'

He debated whether to remember.

'I don't, actually. Sorry.'

'But you heard them talk about it?'

'Yes. I think maybe . . . maybe he was saying something about a film adaptation? I'm not sure . . .'

'Did he say any names – directors, actresses?'

Matthew frowned.

'Gosh, I wish I could remember.'

The detective gave an accommodating shrug.

'Would you say he was trying to pick her up?'

'Yes. Definitely.'

He could sense Chloe flinching beside him. It had been a cruel thing to say, but it was in her interest, as well as his own, to push the story as far away from any connection to her as possible.

Charlie spoke:

'I mean, you guys don't need me to tell you how to do your job, but it might be worth asking the barman if he remembers the book this woman was reading, if you're trying to track her down. Barmen notice that kind of thing.'

The detective gazed at him mildly for a moment.

'That's a good idea.'

'Maybe she could shed some light on this call Grollier got at the bar,' Charlie continued, 'because that's the real question you want answered here, isn't it? And why he left in such a hurry right after?'

'We'd certainly be interested in knowing that.'

'The obvious inference, to me,' Charlie said, 'assuming you haven't traced the call –'

The detective kept his face impassive.

'– is that he was using a cash-only phone, which suggests either he was involved in something criminal, which I highly doubt, or else he was having some kind of clandestine relationship, in which case presumably there'd be traces in the house.'

'Wasn't he living with that actress?' Matthew put in.

'Rachel Turpin, yeah,' Charlie said. 'But people do have affairs, you know. Maybe he was seeing someone up here.' He laughed, pleased at his powers of deduction, and turned to the detective. 'Did you guys think about that? Maybe that's why he was in Aurelia in the first place!'

Chloe, who'd been silent until now, said in a calm voice:

'Then why would he be picking up random women at the Millstream?'

That seemed to flummox Charlie.

'Good point, Chlo. Unless he was just some kind of compulsive philanderer . . .' He turned back to the detective. 'Anyway, all I'm saying, for what it's worth, is I personally don't think this mysterious phone call could have had anything to do with him getting killed. Because what would the scenario be? Someone luring him back to the house in order to murder him, which they did by stabbing him in the throat? That just sounds ridiculous.'

The detective turned to Chloe:

'You say you talked to Mr Grollier at this fundraising event – when was it – two years ago?'

'About that.'

'How would you describe him?'

'Well . . . We didn't talk for long. I actually didn't even remember I'd met him at all till my husband reminded me.'

'Do you remember what you talked about?'

'No. I'm sure it was just, you know, party conversation.'

'And he didn't make any particular impression on you?'

Chloe frowned:

'I seem to remember he was funny.'

'He made you laugh?'

'I guess he must have.'

'Had you seen any of his movies?'

Chloe hesitated fractionally:

'No.'

'But you've seen them since?'

She looked at the detective, seeming to wonder how she'd prompted that question.

Lie, Matthew told her silently.

'Not that I recall,' she said. 'We haven't, have we, Charlie?'

'Definitely not.'

She turned back to the detective:

'I didn't think so.'

'And he never contacted you again after that meeting?'

She looked at Fernandez with an expression of placid indifference, as if she had no idea what he was driving at, and no interest in trying to guess.

'No,' she said.

Attagirl! Matthew wanted to tell her. She'd been nervous, but when it came to it, her performance had been flawless.

The detective finished his coffee and set his mug down on the table next to the Scrabble board. He looked back through the pages of his notebook.

'You know what?' He smiled at each of them. 'I think we're done.'

He put his notepad away.

'You've been extremely helpful. Thank you all.'

He leaned forward to get out of his seat. As he was rising, though, something seemed to stall him. The uniformed officer, who'd been sitting silently in the window seat, had just taken out her handkerchief again and blown her nose. Whether or not that had anything to do with it wasn't clear to Matthew, but some new thought appeared to register itself on the detective's face as he came to a halt, his unfolding body suspended midway between sitting and standing, his balding head angling back down towards the coffee table, staring at it. Slowly, carefully, as though an abrupt move might cause whatever it was he'd thought or seen to vanish, he lowered himself back down into the sofa.

'Although now since we're here, maybe I should ask you just a couple more questions. Save us having to come back further down the road. Would that be okay with you?'

'Of course,' Charlie said. 'We're all extremely eager to get this cleared up. It isn't too relaxing knowing there's a killer wandering around out there. I was actually wondering at what point you call in the big guns – you know, the State police, the FBI, whatever . . .'

Matthew let his eyes drift casually towards the coffee table, wondering what had caught the detective's attention. Could it have been something on the Scrabble board? He scanned the criss-crossing words, but on reflection the idea of a detective picking up some cryptic clue from a Scrabble game seemed unlikely.

'What I'm thinking –' Fernandez was tapping his pen against his notepad – 'is that it would be helpful to have a record of what you were doing yourselves the night Mr Grollier was killed.'

Charlie gave an incredulous snort. 'You mean our alibis?'

'Like I say, it's just so we have it on record,' Fernandez said affably. 'Dotting our I's and crossing our T's so to speak.'

'Of course,' Chloe said politely. She had turned ashen since the detective had sat back down. 'Charlie was in New York having dinner. Matthew and I were here all afternoon. Matthew went out to the Millstream bar – I think around six-thirty, right, Matt?' Matthew nodded. 'And I left about ten minutes later to spend the evening with my cousin Jana in Lake Classon. Our daughter was still away at camp – that's her upstairs practising. I can give you my cousin's number if you like.'

'Thank you. We'll get all your details before we go.'

Might it have been something about the books then? Matthew looked at the lavish monographs and *catalogues raisonnés* of Chloe's favourite photographers as closely

225

as he dared: Nan Goldin, Robert Frank, the Helmut Newton book . . . Was it possible that one of these had some unsuspected suggestion of Grollier about it? But that, too, seemed unlikely. He thought perhaps he'd been imagining things after all, and Fernandez really was just trying to make sure he didn't have to come back unnecessarily.

The detective had turned back to Charlie:

'And just so I have it straight, you came home after your dinner in New York, or you spent the night somewhere in the city?'

'Well, we have a home in the city too, but I came back here.'

'What time did you leave?'

'Around ten. Happy to give you contact details of the people I was with.'

'Thanks. So you got back here, what, around midnight?'

'Yeah, twelve, twelve-thirty,' Charlie said airily.

'Twelve, twelve-thirty,' the detective said, writing in his notepad. 'And went straight to bed?'

'Yes,' Charlie answered.

'Actually, Charlie,' Matthew heard himself say, 'wasn't that the night you had to stop for a nap on the Thruway?'

Charlie looked at him. He'd obviously thought the nap wasn't worth mentioning.

'Oh, yeah, you're right. I'd forgotten that. So it was probably a bit later.'

'So . . . what time then, approximately?' the detective asked.

'Yeah, probably closer to one-thirty, two.'

The detective looked down at his notepad, stroking his moustache for a moment.

'Thanks,' he said, and turned to Matthew.

'And just to go back to the Millstream Inn, sir. You left at what time, approximately?'

'I'd say around seven-fifteen, seven-thirty.'

'But you didn't see Mr Grollier take a call on his phone.'

'No. I think I'd have remembered if I had.'

'Did you go to the fireworks?'

Matthew had already decided there was nothing to gain by pretending he'd been at the fireworks.

'No, I came back here. Got an early night.'

The detective nodded, writing in his pad.

'All right.' He turned to face Chloe and Charlie. 'Now if I could just ask if either of you have plans to travel over the next few days? Just in case we have other questions for you.'

'No,' Charlie said drily. 'We have friends coming to visit. I doubt we'll be leaving the house. Feel free to drop in any time.'

'I'm actually going to New York tomorrow for a few days,' Matthew volunteered. 'I'll be back on Thursday.'

'Okay,' the detective said, without great interest.

He stood up, his glance lingering a moment on the coffee table.

'What's the word for those little orange guys?' he said, pointing at the plate Chloe had brought in earlier. 'My mom used to call them *quinotos* . . .'

'Those? Kumquats,' Charlie said. 'My wife's addicted to them. Kumquats and chocolate together. Preferably in the same bite. Right, Chlo? Help yourself.'

'Maybe I'll take one for the road, and a little piece of chocolate.' The detective took a kumquat and a piece of the dark chocolate.

'Let me just get those contacts from you,' he said. 'Then we'll be out of your hair.'

The uniformed officer took down the contact details. Matthew looked at her, wondering again if she'd seen something, but there was nothing to be gleaned from her blank expression.

It was still raining when they left. Their car, an unmarked black Ford Explorer, sizzled on the wet as it pulled out. A few yellow leaves, fallen from the trees along the driveway, gleamed behind them on the dark-ened gravel.

'Morons,' Charlie said, closing the door.

Chloe looked at him:

'You weren't very polite.'

'I don't grovel to flunkies. Not my style. Anyway, the guy was completely out of line.'

'He was just doing his job.'

'His job? His job is to be down at that Rainbow encampment or over in Crackville or Methville –' those were Charlie's names for the two little run-down communities west of Aurelia where the county's poorest residents lived – 'finding out whose deadbeat neighbour just tricked out his Chevy or came home from Sears with a brand new log-splitter. Not lounging around nice people's houses sipping coffee and pretending to be Hercule Poirot. "Dotting our I's and crossing our T's" . . . For fuck's sake!'

'Calm down, Charlie.' Chloe was clearing off the table now, moving slowly, as if through some thicker element than air. She had the look of an accident victim trying to assess the damage while still absorbing the blow.

'I mean, he seemed to think it was seriously possible we had something to do with this business!'

'I don't think so.'

'Come on, Chlo, he practically accused you of having an affair with the guy.'

Chloe looked at her husband, her face wrung tight. For a terrible instant Matthew thought she was going to crack; spill it all. But she said quietly:

'You're getting carried away, Charlie.'

Charlie glanced at her, holding her gaze for a moment before turning aside with a subdued, sheepish look.

'Sorry.'

'Why don't you take Fu for a walk? He needs exercise.'

'Good idea,' Charlie muttered. 'I could use some air myself.'

Fu came padding in at the sound of his own name, and Charlie clipped on his leash. He'd put on his Burberry rain jacket and was just leading Fu out through the sliding door when he turned back to Matthew.

'By the way, Matt. I thought you were leaving us for good tomorrow. I didn't realise you were coming back.'

'Oh!' Matthew said. 'Well, if you'd rather I didn't . . .'

'No. I'd just forgotten.'

'Of course we want you to come back,' Chloe said, looking sharply at Charlie.

'Of course,' Charlie echoed. 'I'm just saying I'd forgotten. I'll see you later.'

He went out with the dog.

He's upset about me contradicting him in front of Fernandez, Matthew thought, watching Charlie through the glass doors. Well, he'd certainly made Charlie look like a liar. Had he intended to? He hoped not. It was a matter of principle with him not to indulge any feelings of ill-will towards Charlie. Not for Charlie's sake, but his own. His sense of personal dignity was tightly bound up in the disavowal of anything that might have been termed resentment. The position he had taken, from the start, was that he was above such pettiness. He preferred to be thought pragmatic, even coldly detached, than vindictive.

He stared out at his cousin: the tall, straight figure walking away from him, as it always was in Matthew's imagination; the slight stiffness of his bearing conveying, as it always had, Charlie's obstinate sense of the world's being forever in his debt. For a brief moment Matthew allowed himself to recall how he had acquiesced in that sense; unprotestingly handing over his own existence when Charlie had required it of him. *After all, Matt, things are already screwed for you, so you might as well . . .* It was the first time since coming to America, he realised, that he'd permitted himself a direct glance at this incident through the

230

intervening years, but the words came back as clearly as if Charlie had just spoken them.

Lily was still upstairs. Alone with Chloe, Matthew felt an unaccustomed awkwardness. She seemed to be waiting for him to say something about the interview, but it was hard to think of anything that wouldn't sound either too knowing or too bland. He wondered if he should make some comment on her lie about not seeing Grollier's movies. It occurred to him that if he didn't, she might think he was deliberately making things easier for her – effectively colluding in the deception – which in turn might make her wonder why. Maybe that was what she was waiting for: some harmless explanation. He plunged in:

'I thought that was extremely cool of you, telling the detective you hadn't seen Grollier's movies.'

She looked away, but he had a feeling he'd been right.

'Oh . . . I just didn't feel like going into it.'

'That's what I assumed,' Matthew said quickly. 'I'd have felt the same. The guy was obviously just stirring things up for the sake of it. Making insinuations, like Charlie said. Why should you play along with it? I was impressed. It showed real *sangfroid*, as my father would have said.'

She opened her mouth, closed it again, and then said:

'What if I *had* been having an affair with Grollier?'

'Ha!' Matthew exclaimed, trying to sound light-heartedly amused.

'Seriously . . .'

231

'Well . . .'

'I'd be in trouble right now for not having told them, wouldn't I?'

'I guess so. If they found out.'

'They'd find out, don't you think?'

'Why?'

'Like Charlie said, if he was having an affair up here, there'd be traces of it all over the house, wouldn't there? Hair, body fluids . . .'

'I suppose. But they'd have to have some reason to try to match them to any particular individual, wouldn't they? I mean, they couldn't just demand DNA samples from every beautiful woman in Aurelia . . .'

'I imagine they'd figure it out, sooner or later,' Chloe said, ignoring the compliment. 'They aren't actually idiots, whatever Charlie thinks.'

'Well, even if they did, so what? It's not as if it would help solve the murder. Unless you did it yourself!' Matthew laughed.

'All the same I should probably tell them, shouldn't I? I mean, if I *had* been having an affair?'

She was practically confessing. In fact, he wondered if at this point it would even be plausible for him to go on pretending she wasn't. But if he let her talk, he knew he'd have to tell her to go to the cops, or else risk looking shifty himself. It struck him that she probably *wanted* him to tell her to go to the cops; that she was looking to him precisely for reassurance that it was the right thing, and that she shouldn't be afraid. Well, he was damned if he was going to do that.

'Depends if you wanted to get dragged into a murder investigation,' he said. 'Have the affair splashed all over the papers . . . I don't imagine the police would keep it secret for long.'

'I thought they sometimes made deals about that kind of thing . . .'

'That seems highly unlikely. Anyway, since you presumably *weren't* having an affair with the guy and didn't kill him, there's no need to torment yourself, is there?'

Matthew smiled at her as encouragingly as he could, wishing he could just tell her she'd handled the detective impeccably, and that she had nothing to worry about.

She nodded vaguely.

'I should go and shop for dinner,' he said, eager to change the subject. 'Anything you need?'

'No, thanks.'

'I'll make something nice.'

She managed a frail smile.

'You always make something nice, Matt.'

He drove off. At a deer farm by the Thruway that advertised all-season meat, he bought a short loin of venison. She'd told him once that venison was her favourite meat, and he wanted to cook something special for her. He'd begun to think he might not be coming back after all. Not that he felt in any immediate danger, but it seemed tempting fate to come back to Aurelia while the police were – effectively, though they didn't know it – looking for him. Also, Charlie obviously didn't want him around.

* * *

Both cars were gone from the driveway when he got back. He was putting his purchases in the fridge when he saw what had been somehow invisible to him earlier: the little dish of kumquats and chocolates that Chloe had brought out during the game of Scrabble. They'd been on the coffee table, staring him in the face all the time he'd been trying to figure out what the detective had seen. She'd left the same snack in the A-frame. He could see it in his mind's eye, down on the glass table beside the love seat. He'd even been dimly aware of it in the darkness and tumult of his departure, but far from thinking he should get rid of it, he'd thought it added a natural touch to the scenario he'd tried to create, of a random burglary gone wrong. *Quinotos*, he thought, remembering the detective's word . . . Had the guy been deliberately signalling to Chloe that he was on to her? Giving her a chance to tell him about her affair in private? Was that where she'd picked up the idea of some kind of confidentiality deal? In which case, he wondered uneasily, what was she doing right now?

He was still unpacking the food when he heard a car pull up outside. Chloe came into the house. She was wearing a white blouse, grey skirt and blue Mary Janes.

She regarded him a moment, the bones of her face outlined by a shaft of sunlight piercing the trees along the driveway. He smiled at her.

'You look like you've been to a job interview!'

'I went to church. I haven't been for a while.'

'They have services in the afternoon?'

'Yes.'

He turned away, not wanting to look too interested.

'Did you go to confession?' he asked, putting the meat in the fridge.

'Of course.'

'I can't imagine,' he said, 'what someone as saintly as you could possibly find to say inside a confessional.'

'Oh, there's always something.'

He turned back to her.

'Charlie took Lily tubing,' she said. 'They'll be home by six-thirty. We should eat early if that's okay.'

She went out of the kitchen. He heard her open the bar fridge by the drinks cabinet in the living room, before climbing the stairs up to her bedroom.

He wasn't sure what to think. It made a certain amount of sense, he supposed, that she'd go to church. She'd certainly have been in need of relief from the unremitting tension of the last few days, and maybe she'd decided this was a safer bet than going to the police. Priests were sworn to secrecy, as far as he knew. Anyway she'd have been careful about that, knowing her; kept anything identifiable with Grollier out of whatever story she'd told. No doubt there were established formulas she could use without going into details. Father, I've strayed from my vows, or something. The priest would have given her some Hail Marys, and told her to end the affair. And of course, she'd be able to assure him that she already had.

But he had a feeling that she'd been lying to him: that she had in fact just been confessing her affair to Detective Fernandez.

Well, suppose she had? That didn't automatically spell catastrophe. It was even possible, he thought, peering into the murky entanglements of the situation, that it might actually do some good. It would clarify Grollier's connection to the household, which in turn might put an end to further investigation. Even if it didn't, suspicion would naturally fall first on Charlie, as the deceived husband, especially after Charlie's lie about what time he got home the night of the murder, which at the very least would buy Matthew some time, for whatever that was worth. All the same, he realised, he'd feel better if he could convince himself that Chloe really had just gone to church.

He poured himself a stiff gin and tonic. Aside from everything else, he didn't think he could face Charlie, after that little clash earlier, without some alcohol inside him.

There was a SousVide machine in the pantry, that Charlie had given Chloe a couple of years ago, after she'd raved about the food at some French place out in Sag Harbor. Neither of them had learned how to use it, so it had stood on the shelf in its manufacturer's box ever since Chloe had unwrapped it. Matthew, who found the whole SousVide system with its hi-tech pretensions and nasty little cooking bags, thoroughly unappealing, had avoided it all summer despite some strong hints from Charlie. But he'd decided to inaugurate it tonight. Along with the venison itself, it would make a nice parting gesture for Chloe. She'd have no idea that that was what it was until much later, of course, but that was fine. She would look back and remember he'd cooked venison for her, using a troublesome method that he'd never shown any personal interest in mastering, and it would cast him, retroactively, in just the right light of sentimental self-abnegation.

Topping up his drink, he salted the lean crimson meat, vacuum sealed it in one of the plastic pouches, and set it to cook. He'd picked up boysenberries for a compote, a red cabbage to braise with a slab of pig cheek, and potatoes for a herbed *spaetzle*.

At six-thirty the convertible drew up outside, disgorging Charlie and Lily.

Charlie barely greeted him. He glanced at the SousVide machine as he walked past it, but didn't comment.

'I thought I'd set up the SousVide,' Matthew said.

Charlie turned back briefly.

'Oh, that's what that is.'

'I bought some venison.'

'Uh-huh? Chlo likes venison. I'm not crazy about it myself. When are we eating?'

'Shouldn't be long.'

Charlie moved on out through the kitchen and disappeared upstairs, Lily following briskly behind. Matthew didn't know whether to be amused or offended by Charlie's rudeness. It was weirdly crass, but then Charlie had never been one to disguise his feelings, and he was obviously still angry about being contradicted in front of the detective.

Chloe made a little more effort to seem interested in the SousVide when she came down.

'That's exciting,' she said, filling her wine glass.

'Well . . . I hope it lives up to expectations . . .'

She gave a distracted smile. She seemed to have retreated somewhere even deeper inside herself during the last hour. She'd clearly drunk quite a bit too. Not that Matthew was exactly sober himself.

The meat came out of its pouch the same raw burgundy colour it had been when it went in. He'd forgotten that peculiarity of the SousVide. Along with the boysenberries and red cabbage, there was something unnervingly purplish about the whole dish.

'You don't have a blowtorch, do you?' he asked, catching a flicker of dismay on Chloe's face. 'I could sear it . . .'

'I'm sure it'll taste fine.'

'You know what?' Charlie said, looking at it. 'I'm just going to grab some cheese and eat up in my office. I have a ton of work to do before these people come tomorrow. You don't mind, do you, Chlo?'

Chloe looked blankly at her husband, and then shrugged. Under normal circumstances, Matthew felt, she wouldn't have let him get away with that. But she clearly wasn't in a state to confront anyone just now.

She barely said a word throughout the meal, and barely touched her food. Lily gazed at her anxiously.

'Are you okay, Mommy?'

Chloe gave her daughter a helpless look, her eyes wide and searching, as if trying to locate her through some thick mist.

'I'm fine, sweetheart.'

The girl drifted off upstairs.

Alone with Chloe, Matthew said, before he could stop himself:

'Charlie's angry with me, isn't he?'

He could tell at once that Charlie had already talked to her. They must have spoken before Charlie took Lily tubing.

'Is he?' she said. 'About what?'

'I don't know. I should ask him, I suppose.'

She looked away, uncomfortably.

'Well, actually I think I do know,' he said.

'Why?'

'He thinks I was trying to make him look like a liar in front of that detective. Chipping in about his nap on the Thruway.'

'Well . . .' She looked up at him, her eyes settling candidly on his. 'Were you?'

Something in her expression, a look of deliberate challenge, made him think of the things he'd heard her tell Grollier; all that crap about blackmailing Charlie.

'No, I wasn't. It just happened to be the truth.'

'You weren't trying to . . .' She broke off.

'What?'

'I don't know . . . Damage his reputation or something?'

'Huh?'

'Right before his deal goes through?'

So that was what Charlie had thought! As usual his cousin was a degree or two more cunning than him in his thinking. Chloe faced him again.

239

'I mean, it wouldn't be good if his partners knew he'd been brought in for questioning in connection with a murder, would it?'

'Why would I want to spoil his deal?'

'I don't know. Maybe you have something against him?'

She was looking at him more coolly than he liked.

An urge to set her straight seized him. Why *not* tell her? he thought. It wasn't as if keeping the damn thing to himself all these years had done him any good. He'd told no one; not his mother or sister, not even Dr McCubbin. It would have seemed a kind of special pleading, a bid for mercy or – worse – pity, and he'd had too much pride to allow himself that, even as a fourteen-year-old. Pride, courage, dignity . . . All those fine qualities were supposed to be their own reward. But really, what good had they done him? What difference had it made to be a proud wreck, a dignified fuck-up?

'How could I possibly have anything against him?' he said, and then added, with careful nonchalance, 'I mean aside from that business when we were at school together. But that was a million years ago. Besides, I never held it against him.'

'What business?'

'He hasn't told you about it?'

'No.'

'You knew I was thrown out, though?'

'Yes . . . But I didn't think it had anything to do with Charlie.'

She looked a bit apprehensive suddenly, which was certainly better than that coldly appraising stare.

'Ha. That's funny, I thought he would have told you.'

She caught his eye, and he could tell she knew he was being disingenuous. He didn't care, though.

'I mean, it was nothing really, just schoolboy stuff. I wouldn't have mentioned it if I didn't think you already knew . . .'

He paused, savouring the look of alarm on Chloe's face. Something actively malignant seemed to have awoken inside him.

'What are you trying to tell me, Matthew?'

'Nothing at all. I'll stop right now if you don't want to hear it.'

'What did Charlie do?' she said quietly.

'Oh, you know, he'd been through a rough time. His mother had just died. He'd started a year late at this very English school, not knowing anyone, except me of course, but obviously feeling he deserved a place somewhat higher up the social hierarchy. You know how Charlie is. He did rise pretty quickly, but there was a little cabal at the top of our year that he couldn't crack; kids friendly with the year above, which was where girls started – below that it was still all boys – which in turn meant parties and clubs and all that stuff. There was one kid, some sort of delinquent aristo with access to high-grade drugs, who kept the group supplied till he was busted smoking a joint in St James's Park, and the headmaster expelled him. Charlie stepped into the breach.'

'Dealing?'

'Yes. Right away, before he even knew where he could procure anything, he let it be known to this group that he was open for business. This all happened in the period right after my father's disappearance, by the way. Our household had been turned upside down. My mother could barely put a sandwich together for our meals. My sister, who was supposed to be going to university, went off to live with some Anglican nuns instead. I was just in a sort of zombie state most of the time, too confused to know what I was feeling. Helping Charlie find a supplier seemed a perfectly natural thing to do. I took him to the Kensington Market which was this place full of Goths and punks and old grey-haired hippies. We were offered grass right away and for a while Charlie just bought the stuff there and resold it at school for a small profit. But then he realised he could do better buying it wholesale. Also people were asking for other things – speed, acid, coke . . . Anyway, we persuaded the guy we were buying from to introduce us to his dealer—'

'We? You were partners in this?'

'No, not really. I was more like his assistant, his gofer. Or maybe "apprentice" would be the word, given the illustrious career I went on to later. We'd fetch the stuff from our new friend Rudy out in Hounslow together and bag it up in my bedroom, and sometimes I'd be the one who actually handed it over to the kids buying it. But it was his operation. All the money was his – incoming as well as outgoing. Anyway, there was this girl in the year above who bought a tab of acid from Charlie. Henrietta Vine. She dropped it at a birthday party in Manchester Square and ran out into Oxford

Street on her way home while she was hallucinating. She thought the buses and taxis were weightless as balloons.'

He paused again, aware of the tension in Chloe's body in her chair opposite him.

'What happened to her?'

'She was hit by a taxi. She had both legs broken and most of her ribs cracked. The school moved quickly to find out where she'd got hold of the stuff. It didn't take long for our names to come up.'

'Yours and Charlie's?'

'Yes.'

'But . . . Charlie wasn't thrown out?'

'No.'

'Why not?'

'Why do you think?'

She looked uncomprehendingly at him a moment, until it dawned on her.

'He got you to take the blame?'

Matthew shrugged.

'Well, as Charlie said when we were told to report to the headmaster's office, "After all, Matt, things are already screwed for you, so you might as well."'

She was staring at him, her eyes very wide, and he stared back, feeling the words go in hard and deep.

'And . . . you agreed?'

'It seemed reasonable to me.'

'Reasonable?'

'I mean, I'd have been kicked out anyway, so why not at least try to save Charlie's skin? There was no point both of us going down if we didn't have to, was there?'

'Why you, though? Why not him?'

'Oh, because he was right. Things *were* already screwed for me.'

His voice had started thickening, he realised. Telling her the story was having an unexpected effect on him. It was as if he were hearing it himself for the first time, and only now grasping the full extent of its implications.

He looked away; unsure, suddenly, if he was speaking out of a wish to avenge himself on Charlie or just, somehow, to account for himself to Chloe. Maybe the two had become inseparable.

'That's what the whole incident made clear – really for the first time,' he said, managing a dry smile. 'I hadn't actually seen my father's disappearance as quite the unmitigated disaster it was until Charlie pointed it out, if you can believe it. But he was right. So yes, I agreed to take the blame.'

He cleared his throat.

'But, you know . . . It's all water under the bridge as far as I'm concerned. Extremely ancient water under an extremely far-off bridge.'

Chloe looked acutely distressed.

'Oh, Matthew,' she said. It wasn't much, but it seemed to him he'd never heard anything quite so sympathetically anguished in his life; not on his behalf. He'd never wanted pity – hers or anyone else's – and he hoped that wasn't what she was feeling now. But whatever emotion was filling her eyes with that look of infinite tenderness, it seemed to be doing him good.

In the silence that followed, he became aware of a familiar ticking sound behind him, in the entranceway to the kitchen. He turned around. Charlie was standing there. Judging from his posture, fully immobile, and utterly silent except for the ticking of his Patek Philippe, he'd been there for some time. Chloe must have seen him appear and decided to let him listen. He looked right through Matthew. Chloe spoke:

'You never told me any of that, Charlie.'

A scoffing sound came from Charlie.

'You should have told me,' Chloe said.

Abruptly, Charlie stepped forward into the room, grabbing his rain jacket.

'I'm going into town to get something decent to eat,' he said. 'I'll see you later.'

He strode out through the front door, slamming it behind him.

'Charlie!' Chloe shouted. A moment later she ran out after him. Matthew could hear her calling Charlie's name in the rain, then the slam of a car door and Chloe yelling, her voice louder than he'd ever heard it: 'Don't you dare! Don't you dare, Charlie!' followed by the pounding of a fist on the car roof: hard enough to dent the panelling, by the sound of it. Charlie must have got out of the car then: Matthew heard the car door close again, more quietly, and Charlie's voice, very controlled, saying: 'I don't have to defend myself against that little shit,' followed by Chloe, her voice audibly constricted with rage, answering: 'You'd better, Charlie, or you'll regret it.' There was a long pause, then Charlie's voice hissed: 'Not here.' Matthew heard their brisk footsteps crunch on the gravel as they walked around the side of the house. A few minutes later they came in through the glass doors and went silently upstairs. For some time, as he cleared up the kitchen, Matthew heard voices through the ceiling. He'd never heard them fight before, and would have liked to hear what they said, but he couldn't make it out. Still, the anger in Chloe's muffled voice was unmistakable, and it seemed to him inconceivable that there weren't going to be some painful repercussions for Charlie, down the line. Chloe might be capable of loving a man she was betraying, but he seriously doubted she'd be able to go on living with a man she despised. And how, he wondered, allowing himself for the first time a steely satisfaction in what his words had surely wrought, how could she not despise Charlie after this? He felt as though he'd discharged himself of some indissolubly corrosive substance. Now let it spread its ruin somewhere else.

It was still raining when he went to bed. The pines stood dripping behind the guest house, dark and immense. Glittering strings ran from the unguttered octagonal eaves. He opened the door and slid the suitcase out from under the bed, half-expecting, as he always did, the things inside to have rearranged themselves, so bristlingly volatile had they become in his imagination. They lay exactly as he had left them. Still, that was something to look forward to: getting rid of this junk. It made him nervous having it there. Several times he'd been on the verge of taking it out; bringing it to the town landfill with the rest of the household garbage. But the thought of some dogged detective or beady-eyed municipal worker spotting something had held him back. Better to dump it all in the city.

It came to him as he lay in bed that he should put the knife in Charlie's safe.

The idea filled him with a strange delight. He pictured the knife lying there, where the Tiffany bracelet had lain at the beginning of the summer. There was something apt and satisfying about the image. It was where Charlie himself would have put it, he decided, if he really had killed Grollier: stashed it there till he came up with a foolproof spot to get rid of it once and for all. Or no, perhaps he'd want to keep it there: hold onto it as some sort of perverse souvenir; the next best thing to the actual scalp of his wife's lover . . .

He imagined Detective Fernandez turning up in Cobble Hill after an anonymous tip-off, armed with a warrant; Charlie's disdainful grin as he showed him the safe and keyed in the date of his mother's death; the look turning to bewilderment as the steel door opened . . . That would be a sight to behold! But of course I'd be long gone by then, Matthew remembered . . . That seemed to be an indispensable element in the idea taking shape in him; the sense of himself radically elsewhere, under a hot blue sky in some place well out of reach of Detective Fernandez and the East Deerfield Sheriff's Department. Because Charlie, knowing Charlie, would surely wriggle out of it one way or another, and sooner

247

or later the trail would resume its original course and destination.

Not that you could physically disappear anymore. That option, such a primordial human yearning, had gone the way of those off-the-grid backwaters that had once made it possible. But you could still vanish by becoming someone else. There'd been endless talk about that when his father ran off. People had suggested he might have found his way to Belize or somewhere in Southeast Asia; acquired a false passport through one of the document-forging operations in Port Loyola or Bangkok, and started life afresh in some tropical hideaway.

Why not follow in his father's footsteps? The idea had a certain inexorable logic about it, after all, or at least a certain fateful appeal. And it wasn't as if he hadn't thought about it before. It had been present in his mind intermittently throughout his adult life; a fantasy of familial reconvergence that had often comforted him in times of stress.

Of course, there was the little matter of money to consider. His father had had the equivalent of well over a million dollars with him when he disappeared, whereas Matthew, when he last checked, had a little under five grand. The disparity made him smile in the darkness of his room. What a failure he was, compared to his old man! How petty and unambitious the field of his own endeavours!

It was only at this juncture in these drifting nocturnal ruminations, that what might have been obvious from the start, had he been more willing to accept the role of vengeful malcontent that life seemed so eager to confer upon him, became apparent. Not that the timing of it altered its complexion in any fundamental way; he was aware of that. But it meant something to him that the idea hadn't been premeditated.

The money would come from Charlie's safe.

The knife would go in and the money would come out.

It was so simple, and so obvious, that the registering of it felt almost irrelevant; as if it had been arranged long ago by providence, and had always been going to happen, whether or not he knew it in advance.

He saw, in his mind's eye, the blocks of cash in the shadows behind the Cipro bottles, stacked in towers of different heights like their own little Financial District. A million and a half dollars: wasn't that what Charlie had told him?

He remembered how disappointed Charlie had seemed by his reaction to the sight of all that 'moolah'. He'd seemed to want Matthew to be impressed, and so Matthew had obligingly pretended to be. But in the peculiar mood that had risen in him now – a sort of euphoric clairvoyance – it occurred to him that perhaps Charlie had wanted something else too: that he'd wanted him not just to be impressed by the money, but to *take* it.

Was that possible? Was that, at some half-conscious level, why Charlie forgot the bracelet in the first place and had Matthew go back and open the safe and see what it contained? Had he been *offering* me the money? Matthew wondered. Hoping I'd scoop it up and disappear out of his life once and for all? Was Matthew's failure to do so the real reason why Charlie was sending him back to the house now?

Absurd! And yet there was something persuasive about the notion; an insidious plausibility that seemed to require him to weigh it seriously in his mind.

Because Charlie owed him; there was no doubt about that. And Charlie knew it, too. He surely remembered as well as Matthew those words he'd spoken as they crossed the schoolyard to the headmaster's office a quarter-century ago. Or even if he'd forgotten the words themselves, he couldn't have forgotten the intent behind them. Because he'd certainly given every indication of *regretting* that intent. Even of wanting forgiveness for it. God knows he'd been eager enough to fork over the little loans Matthew had been compelled to ask for at moments of desperation over the years; often throwing in a few hundred dollars extra as if to convey his awareness that it was he, Charlie, who was getting the real relief from these transactions, the real easing of burdens. . . And judging from his behaviour these past few weeks, he'd have been happy, more than happy, to make one last act of contrition in order to secure the permanent disappearance of his problematic cousin.

A million and a half dollars. It wouldn't seriously harm Charlie, but it was a decent sum. Not excessive, considering the fact that, in addition to everything else, Matthew had also done Charlie the favour (he hadn't seen it in quite this way before, but it was indisputable now that he thought of it) of eliminating his wife's lover. But certainly an acceptable sum. A person could surely get whatever it took to start life afresh, with a million and a half bucks, and still have plenty left over. It wasn't as if he intended to be idle. He'd go somewhere quiet, low key. Buy a place with a little land. Find some locals to go into business with. Plant gardens and orchards with them; raise chickens and goats. He'd always liked the idea of a communal enterprise; the company of some like-minded people to nourish the spirit and soften the drudgery of work. He'd accepted too unprotestingly the isolating conditions of work in London and then New York; the ethos of every man for himself. His new life would be more open-hearted, more spacious and purposeful than the mere getting-by he'd settled for in the past. He'd always known there was something narrow and aimless, something wearyingly selfish, in the way he'd gone about things in the past. An absence of thought for anything beyond the limits of his own immediate wants and needs. It was never the life he would have chosen, but choice had never seemed a very serious component in his existence. You just grabbed what you could from the few things that presented themselves. Even when he'd gone in with those others – an entertainment lawyer, a couple who invested in artisanal food start-ups, a former City Hall official who knew how to oil the wheels of the city's permit bureacracy – on that farm-to-table project, they'd each been in it purely for

251

their own private gain. It was just business; only ever just business, which was perhaps why it hadn't excited him in the end, even though he'd made a little money out of it.

Well, here was his opportunity to do things differently. To be a better person; live a more generous life! Wasn't that what he wanted, more than anything? Wasn't it what everybody wanted? He could work hard; physically as well as mentally: he knew that. Everyone could work hard under the right conditions, and it was possible to enjoy hard work, even the most numbing, back-breaking toil. But you had to have a sense of participating in some greater good than just the maintaining of your own small existence; some human quorum or congregation of a size sufficient to align you *with* the world instead of against it. The imagination had to be fired, and kept alight. The heart had to feel the presence of joy and warmth. He saw that very clearly now, and for a moment he seemed to see himself as if in a dream-like film, surrounded by kindred spirits at the warm centre of some bustling enterprise in which food, wine, starlight, warm breezes and the sounds of human conviviality combined like the elements of some ancient ceremony to plunge the parched spirit back into the flow of life's inexhaustible abundance.

It struck him that in a peculiar way the difficulties he'd hoped to resolve during his stay up here in Aurelia were being resolved, now, in spite of everything. Perhaps even *because* of everything! It was a strange thought: that in order to win this reprieve, he'd had to do precisely the things he had done. That killing Grollier was, in fact,

the necessary condition for this second chance at life . . .
A vertiginous thought. And yet it, too, seemed to have
something dimly plausible about it. In the darkness of
the little guest house with the dwindling rain pattering
erratically on the shingle roof, it seemed to him he might
have just stumbled, rather late in life (and very late in
comparison with his cousin Charlie), on some fundamental secret about happiness and fulfilment.

He knew where he was going to go, of course. He
hadn't been there since he was a boy, but as he lay
thinking of it now it was as vivid to him as though he'd
been living there all his life. He saw the bustling port
with its pink customs building and wooden houses
drowning in hibiscus and frangipani. He remembered
the narrow cement road that wound up through the old
coconut plantations into hills where the air smelled of
goats and nutmeg and woodsmoke. He thought of the
little restaurant high above the yacht harbour where
they'd sit on the balcony every afternoon, counting the
different blues of the bay and watching the sinking sun
throw javelins of shadow through the forest of masts.
There was no airstrip on the island, and at that time there
was no ferry either, and the journey itself was one of the
highlights of the holiday, with its combination (irresistible to a schoolboy) of luxury and inconvenience. They'd
fly to Barbados, then squeeze into a series of successively
smaller planes and air taxis until they arrived on the
neighbouring island where, as night fell, they'd board
the 'schooner' (an old wooden banana boat) to their own
island, sharing the broad-planked deck with islanders

carrying caged guinea fowl and sacks of mangoes and soursops. Once they'd reached the open sea, the crew would raise two rust-coloured sails that bellied out enormously in the warm breeze, and the rest of the journey would pass without any engine racket, just the bubbling of their wake and the chatter of island voices with their beautiful, lilting English. The stars would come out and after an hour they'd start to see the glitter of the little port and catch that sweet fragrance from the hills, and the feeling of imminent adventure would be almost overwhelming.

Drifting to sleep he saw the blue-shuttered Tranqué Bay Hotel where they'd wake to the brilliance of the Caribbean morning, and race each other past the old stone ruins to the beach. It was there, after they'd swum and breakfasted, and installed themselves on deckchairs in the shade of the stately palms, that his father would look up at the turquoise house on the hillside across the bay, half-hidden in foaming blossoms, and announce that if the family ever came into any serious money, *that* was the house he would buy.

Well, the family was about to come into some serious money.

Thirteen

He woke early. The air was moist, cluttered with scents from the wet trees and some late-blooming roses. He breathed in deeply as he walked down the little rocky path. It was his last day at the house: he was sure of that now, and he felt a sentimental wish to supply himself with good things to remember about it. The air, always so fresh and sweet compared to Bushwick, was one of those things.

Chloe was in the utility room off the kitchen, putting sheets in the dryer. She straightened up, hearing him come in.

'Hi, Matthew.'

There were dark circles under her eyes. She and Charlie had still been quarrelling when he went to bed last night. He was curious to hear what Charlie'd had to say for himself, though he didn't feel he should ask directly. Chloe was looking at him, her expression a little uncomfortable, as if she had something difficult to report but wasn't sure how to broach it.

'Want some breakfast?' he asked airily. 'I thought I'd make shirred eggs.'

'Actually, I was wondering if I could ask you a favour?'

'Of course.'

'Would you mind running into town and picking up some pastries? It's just that we have to get the place ready for these visitors, and Shelley's away, so I thought we'd keep the cooking to a minimum.' Shelley was the cleaner.

'No problem.'

'Thanks, Matt.'

He drove into town, reluctant to believe this errand was really all she'd had on her mind. She'd wanted to talk about Charlie, he sensed, but had qualms about doing it. Which suggested she'd had something less than flattering to say about her husband. In other words it was all exactly as he had predicted! The only surprise was how quickly the process had begun. It crossed his mind that Chloe had spent the night in the guest room, too appalled by what she'd learned about Charlie to sleep with him. He quelled an impulse to rejoice, but he couldn't pretend he wasn't gratified by the idea of Charlie's domestic contentment being shattered.

He pulled in behind the hardware store, parking by their fleet of hydraulic machines – diggers, augers, log-splitters, leaf-mulchers – that stood along the rental section like strange, demonic beasts. Early-to-Bread was busy, and it was several minutes before his turn came at the register. He ordered the usual selection of muffins and scones and took them back to the truck.

There was no sign of life in the house when he got back. He arranged the pastries on a dish at the centre of the kitchen table and went to the guest house. His bus didn't leave Aurelia till two in the afternoon but he thought he might as well get his packing done. It didn't take long. As he looked around the octagonal room one last time, it occurred to him he could replicate it where he was going. Not the view, of course – he'd be looking over the sapphire waters of Tranqué Bay or somewhere like it, assuming all went well – but the furnishings and the rough plank walls. And maybe there *would* be a view of a pool through one of the windows some day, with a butterfly garden next to it just like Chloe's. At this thought the image of Chloe herself, charged by the realisation that he wouldn't be seeing her again, flooded him with an emotion so intense she seemed almost palpably present in the room, and for a moment he had the impression that he could smell her scent, and that if he were to reach out he could touch her living hand.

As he wheeled his suitcase through the pool gate, she came out of Charlie's meditation garden, carrying her phone.

'Oh, hi,' she said, putting the phone away. 'You're back.'

He smiled, feeling the familiar jolt of re-entry as he passed from that realm of secret communion with her to the plane of ordinary conversation.

'I put the pastries on the kitchen table,' he said.

She thanked him vaguely, and offered to reimburse him.

'Don't be silly.'

She was looking even more uncomfortable than she had before.

'Listen, Matthew . . .'

He tilted his head sympathetically; convinced he was finally about to hear that his story last night had forced some fundamental reappraisal of the man she was married to. But he was wrong again.

'I've just found out there's a direct bus from East Deerfield at nine-thirty,' she said, speaking quickly. 'I need to go in this morning anyway, so I thought maybe I should take you to that instead of the later one. How would that be? It'll save us having to go out again in the afternoon, and it'll also be a much quicker journey for you . . .'

She sounded nervous, he thought. She must have been afraid he'd be upset about being turfed out early. But he was actually relieved not to have to linger. Aside from giving him more time in New York to organise himself, it would get him out of having to confront Charlie before he left, which he'd been dreading.

'Whatever's easiest for you.'

'We'd have to leave right away.'

'No problem. I'm all packed. I just need the key.'

She looked blank.

'To your house. I'm staying there.'

'Oh. Right. I'll get it.'

She went ahead of him, moving briskly while he wheeled his suitcase over the lawn, and met him in the kitchen with the Cobble Hill keys.

258

'Charlie's still in bed, but . . .'

'That's okay. I'll see him on Thursday.' It seemed important to maintain the fiction that he was going to be returning later in the week. 'Assuming I'm allowed back . . .'

He smiled ruefully, hoping the remark might finally get them on to the topic of last night's row. But she didn't respond, and as soon as they got into the Lexus she started her infuriating humming once again, the soft drone as effective a barrier to conversation as a diving bell would have been. She kept it up all the way through Aurelia and onto the County Road beyond. He gazed out through the window, doing his best to ignore both the humming itself and the insensitivity it seemed to imply. Small houses straggled from the outskirts of town: dilapidated old clapboard cottages and the vinyl-sided bungalows referred to, in the optimistic American parlance, as 'ranch' houses, as if they had a thousand head of cattle round the back. His mind went to his cramped apartment in Bushwick, with its living-room window facing a wall, and a momentary gloom descended on him until he remembered he wasn't going to be living there anymore. The new life he'd charted out last night seemed to be only fitfully present in his mind. He concentrated, trying to make it more real for himself.

Still humming, Chloe turned onto Route 39, the busy highway into East Deerfield. He couldn't help feeling a little hurt by her uncommunicativeness. He'd bared his soul to her, after all, and she'd obviously been moved by what he'd told her. At the very least, he thought, she owed it to him to reveal what Charlie had had to say for himself. Had he professed any guilt about his actions? Matthew wondered. Any remorse? Not that it would make any material difference at this point, but he'd have liked to know. He stared out again, watching the familiar old landmarks reel past: gravel quarry; furniture liquidation store, Swedish Auto . . . As they loomed up and disappeared, he tried to impress on himself that it was the last time he'd be seeing any of them; that this phase of his life, the American phase, was over. Here were the unfinished McMansions of a residential development abandoned after the financial meltdown, plywood walls blackening under peeling skins of Tyvek. Charlie liked to point these out as an example of why bankers needed to be regulated. 'Repealing Glass-Steagall,' he'd declare in that righteous way of his, 'was the banking equivalent of legalising assault weapons.' It occurred to Matthew that Charlie, too, had disappeared out of his life for the last time; striding out through the kitchen last night and slamming the door behind him.

'So what did Charlie have to say about what I told you?' he blurted, unable to contain himself any longer.

Chloe stopped humming. They'd reached the traffic circle outside East Deerfield and she slowed down, taking the exit for the bus station. He saw the tip of her tongue dart out to moisten her lips.

'You mean about the . . . thing at your school?'

'Yes.'

She paused for a long moment before answering, and kept her eyes steadily on the road as she finally spoke.

'He said you were lying.'

Matthew was too stunned to speak for a moment. It was as though Charlie had just punched him in the face.

'What?' he said.

'He said you'd made the whole thing up.'

'My God! Did you believe him?'

'No. I told him I thought that would be totally out of character for you.'

'Thank you,' he said, hugely relieved. 'And what did he say to that?'

Chloe glanced in the mirror, but stared forward immediately, as if avoiding his eye. He understood: she'd been put in an extremely awkward position, effectively having to choose between himself and her husband. No wonder she'd been looking so uncomfortable earlier. Still, at least she'd had the decency to abide by her own instinct for the truth. It certainly would have been easier to go along with Charlie's monstrous little invention. She answered him, speaking with a kind of wavering but determined firmness:

'He said you were a crook. He . . . he said you always had been.'

'Christ! That's a bit desperate, isn't it?'

'He said you'd been stealing things from him all summer . . .'

'You're kidding! What things?'

She swallowed. She was gripping the steering wheel tightly, he noticed; her knuckles bright as candle flames.

'Oh, little things . . . A pair of cufflinks. Some money from his wallet. He said he'd seen you eyeing his father's

261

watch by the pool one day, like you were planning to take that too.'

'I don't believe it! Don't you think he'd have mentioned that earlier if it was true?'

'I told you, I didn't believe him. We had a big fight about it, in case you didn't notice.'

Matthew nodded. They stopped at a red light. Chloe stared forward in silence. He could see the vein in her neck pulsating in sharp throbs. She'd closed her mouth and was breathing in deeply through her nose as if to steady herself. The light went green and as they moved forward she spoke again:

'He said the reason he didn't mention it earlier was that he felt sorry for you.'

'Christ almighty!'

'Personally I think—'

She broke off. The bus station came into view ahead, the grimy white pillars of its open hangar gleaming in the sunlight.

'You think . . .' Matthew prompted her.

'I think it was because he felt guilty.'

'For what he did at school?'

'Yes.'

It took a moment for the implications of this to sink in.

'Wait, you're not saying you believe him, though, are you? You don't actually think I stole from him, do you?'

They'd reached the bus station. She pulled in and found a space at the back of the parking lot. She seemed extremely agitated, her small upper teeth biting down on one side of her lip as she manoeuvred into the space.

'Your bus is here. You'd better hurry,' she said. Her voice was breathy and he could hear a distinct tremor in it.

'I'm confused, though, Chloe . . . You're not saying *you* think I lied or . . . or stole from him, are you?'

'Go on. You'll miss your bus.'

'But, Chloe . . .'

'Get out, Matthew!' she said, turning to him with sudden savagery.

He opened the door, his confusion seeming to migrate to his legs as he climbed out and took his suitcase from the trunk. As he rolled it to the front of the car to say goodbye she pulled forward with an abrupt lurch.

'Chloe!' he called.

She stopped, just as abruptly, a few yards off from him. As he moved towards her he saw she was rummaging in her canvas bag. She thrust something towards him as he reached her window.

'You stole *this*,' she said. 'Didn't you?'

It was the gold-and-quartz Montblanc pen he'd found in their sofa.

'I looked in your suitcase,' she said. 'Just now when I sent you into town. I had to know if Charlie was lying to me.'

'Oh.' His voice came like a strange sigh.

'It wasn't all I found.'

He seemed to feel all the strength sluice out of him.

'You were in the house that whole time, weren't you?'
Her face had darkened in blotches, contorted. She seemed
barely able to speak. The pen was shaking in her hand
like the needle on some dangerously overburdened meas-
uring instrument. 'You'd gone there to watch us, hadn't
you?'

'No! That isn't—'

'And then you killed him.'

'That's not what happened. Wait, Chloe—' She'd
started pulling away again. 'I'll tell you what happened—'

'I was nice to you is what happened,' Chloe said.

He wanted to tell her everything suddenly. It seemed
to him she'd understand. If anyone could understand, it
was Chloe. But she'd pressed the window button and
the glass was sliding up between them.

'Chloe—'

'I hope you rot in hell, Matthew.'

She'd reached the parking-lot exit.

'Chloe!' he called after her, his mind reeling. The
window had closed. He watched her ease the car back
into the traffic and drive off. For several seconds he was
unable to move. Immense forces seemed to be pressing
down, immobilising him. It was as if the moment were
too densely freighted with reality to pass through. He
heard her words again: *I hope you rot in hell* . . . She
knew what he had done, and her knowing it seemed to
make it real for the first time. He had killed Grollier,
taken his life. A feeling of horror surged inside him. The
stark fact seemed to lie all around him suddenly, like
some vast, untraversable desert. And yet, he thought,

trying to steady himself, she'd brought him here, hadn't she? She'd brought him here to the bus station, and that surely meant something. She could have called the cops to the house, told them what she'd seen, but she'd brought him here instead. So maybe she *had* understood in some way; seen that he wasn't to blame for it; that Grollier, no less than himself, had been *Charlie's* fall guy, one more surrogate for Charlie's pain. Or maybe it was just that she was so intent on keeping her affair a secret from Charlie she'd chosen to pretend not to have seen what she'd seen. Either way she'd let him go, hadn't she? Told him she knew what he'd done, told him to rot in hell, but let him go. Well then, he thought, moving forward, he owed it to her to make it work.

Buses were lined up either side of the outdoor shelter, engines throbbing, fumes spewing out into the morning air. He'd be in New York in a few hours, he told himself; on a plane as soon as possible after that. Meanwhile he needed to get a ticket, a bottle of water, something to eat. He passed between the buses, focusing determinedly on his objective as he breathed their acrid stench: Tranqué Bay, the land he was going to buy with Charlie's 'moolah', the turquoise house on the hill. Dimly, as he came out into the open forecourt, he became aware of something encroaching on him, some vague darkness that seemed more an emanation of the horror still present inside him than anything external. He ignored it, keeping his mind on the vision he'd had the night before, of a new exist-ence, the new person he was going to become. He made himself think of the joy of those sparkling mornings, racing past the old stone ruins to the beach and plunging into the waves with the smell of salt air filling his lungs and the palms along the shoreline tossing in the breeze as if in their own raptures of delight. People were jostling around him; passengers going in and out of the ticket office, taxi drivers looking for fares, officials from the bus company. Again the sense of some encroaching darkness intruded; a shape that was somehow both a solid object entering his field of vision and at the same time a kind of blackly spectral embodiment of what he had done, looming back on a surge of renewed horror. He focused tenaciously on the bright image, as if the sheer glittering intensity of it, pictured with sufficient conviction, might be enough to draw him forward through the many obstacles and difficult passages that lay ahead.

He was still seeing it in his mind's eye when the black Ford Explorer that had emerged from behind the ticket office and been slowly approaching him all this while, came to a halt a few feet off. The doors opened, but even as Detective Fernandez climbed out and strolled calmly towards him followed by Officer Lombardi, it was some time before he was able to adjust from the glare of that sunlit future, and understand what was happening.